Ashraf El-Ashmawi is an Egyptian author, judge, and legal scholar. He is a regular contributor to newspapers and online publications. He has written eleven novels that have been critically received: longlisted for the International Prize for Arabic Fiction; best novel at the Cairo International Book Fair; and winner of best novel at the Bahrain Cultural Forum. His books have been translated into multiple languages and *The House of the Coptic Woman* is his second novel to be translated into English, following *The Lady of Zamalek*.

Peter Daniel, a long-term resident of Egypt, has worked as a teacher of Arabic as a foreign language and an Arabic-to-English translator for many years.

T0000957

The House of
the Coptic Woman

Ashraf El-Ashmawi

Translated by
Peter Daniel

hoopoe
AN IMPRINT OF AUC PRESS

First published in 2023 by
Hoopoe
113 Sharia Kasr el Aini, Cairo, Egypt
420 Lexington Avenue, Suite 1644, New York, NY 10170
www.hoopoefiction.com

Hoopoe is an imprint of The American University in Cairo Press
www.aucpress.com

ISBN 978 1 649 03254 6

Library of Congress Cataloging-in-Publication Data

Names: 'Ashmāwī, Ashraf, author. | Daniel, Peter (Translator),
    translator.
Title: The house of the coptic woman : a novel / Ashraf El-Ashmawi, Peter
    Daniel.
Other titles: Bayt al-Qibṭīyah. English
Identifiers: LCCN 2023016659 | ISBN 9781649032546 (trade paperback) |
ISBN   9781649032539 (hardback) | ISBN 9781649032553 (epub) | ISBN
9781649032560 (adobe pdf)
Subjects: LCGFT: Thrillers (Fiction) | Legal fiction (Literature) | Novels.
Classification: LCC PJ7914.S475 B3913 2023 | DDC
    892.7/37--dc23/eng/20230607

1 2 3 4 5   27 26 25 24 23

Designed by Adam el-Sehemy

To those who lived in my imagination for many years: the Arabic language instructor Hoda Yusef Habib, the guard Nabawi el-Dib, the peacock warden Mohammed Alwan, the itinerant salesman Labib, the electricity company employee Halim Iskander Tadros, the child Hamada Islam, the farmer Naguib Samuel, and the carpet trader Hilal Khidr. May they all rest in peace.

1

DROWSINESS SLOWLY SEDUCED MY EYELIDS. I listlessly resisted. The tug-of-war lasted until the car took a sharp swerve to the far right of the highway. I took stock of my surroundings. Dark autumnal clouds raced overhead, surging and swelling, threatening rain, only to retreat at the last moment. They withdrew, dispersing as the looming night laid siege and eventually engulfed them.

I lowered the window for a blast of cold air to invigorate me. I shuddered and cranked the window closed again, tightly. My whole body started to jig-jog as the tarmac gave way to rugged, unpaved roads with nothing but fields on either side. The headlights hit a sign so corroded by rust that I could barely make it out. "Tayea Village," it announced in an elegant script, or what was left of it. I tapped the driver on the shoulder.

"Do we have much more to go?"

He nodded toward an old building, two-thirds hidden behind tall camphor trees, and turned left.

"We're here, sir."

The driver took my bags from the trunk and, preceding me with broad strides, disappeared behind some trees. Since they were not very successful at hiding the rest house, nightfall dutifully lent a hand, lowering its dark curtains to shroud it until dawn. I felt my heart sink as I approached what would be my new residence for the coming year. It looked forsaken. Beneath the faint light of the eclipsed moon, I faced a small colonial style villa, a two-storey affair with paint chipping off the walls and sloping eaves covered with terracotta tiles. There was a large front yard hemmed in by a wooden fence low enough for me to jump over, so I jumped, feeling the thrill of a mischievous kid.

I noticed two smaller structures near the edge of the grounds. From the similarity of their design, I assumed they served the villa. Loud barks pierced the silence, followed by the grumbles and curses of what was probably a tied-up dog. A man must've pelted it with a stone or two to shut it up since the barking soon grew sporadic then stopped.

"Welcome to *Tayha*, sir. You've lit up the whole village."

The deliverer of this rustic greeting emerged from behind a thick copse. As he strode toward me, a neutral smile gradually broadened into a wide grin. I was surprised by how he pronounced the name of the village. But then, of course, he knew its story as well as I did.

I studied his face beneath the lantern he held. Well past middle age, his hair had grayed but had not receded much. Judging from his build, he seemed of modest health, fit only for the bare necessities of life. He had a long hooked nose which suited his bony, hunched torso atop long and skinny legs. The remnants of his rather disconcerting smile remained fixed on his face even as he spoke. This must be Ramses, the lodge's elderly caretaker. A fellow public prosecutor had mentioned him a couple of weeks ago when he explained to me what my life would be like in this village on the outskirts of a provincial town. I had been appointed to replace that colleague in this post with no advance warning and despite the fact that I'd been with the public prosecution less than three years.

The driver drove off, leaving the loud grumbles of an ancient motor in his wake. As the noise faded, Ramses picked up my suitcase, easily carrying its weight despite his frail physique. He led the way with the confident strides of an honor guard. I was struck by a sense of foreboding as I approached the front steps, which eventually subsided as Ramses switched on the lights.

As soon as I stepped inside, my attention was drawn to an enormous oak bookcase. It covered two walls from floor to ceiling, yet it was almost entirely empty, if it were not for the thick layers of dust, some scarce reference works on criminal law, and multiple volumes of *The Principles of the Court of Cassation*, which were immediately recognizable from their hefty size and the poor quality of their dark brown and green bindings. Somehow I detected two much smaller and slimmer books tucked between the legal tomes. From their size and binding, I could tell they were not remotely connected to law. I was intrigued. I gently worked them free only to discover they were both by Tawfiq al-Hakim. The first was his famous novel, *Diary of a Country Prosecutor*, and the second, *Justice and Art*, a collection of autobiographical stories from his career as a public prosecutor, which had attracted little attention when it first appeared.

"Those books have been here for fifty years or more. Nobody reads them," Ramses said, interrupting my thoughts.

Fifty years? I smiled as I imagined Tawfiq al-Hakim himself serving as a public prosecutor in this very village. I pictured him, putting pen to paper, writing these works right here in this room, then leaving them on the bookshelf for his successors to read and take heed.

I turned to inspect the rest of the place as though on a first visit to a crime scene. At the other end of the room stood a dining table large enough to seat nine, with one end shoved against the wall. I lifted a corner of the grimy plastic table cloth to find the wood in poor condition. I let the tablecloth fall back into place with a shrug. I suddenly felt very weary. I turned to Ramses and asked, "Where's my room?"

"Choose whichever you please, sir. We have four large bedrooms here. Each has a large balcony to relax on and its own bathroom with a—um—sit-down toilet, if you'll excuse the expression, sir."

"Yes, I see. But what about the other judicial officials who are staying here?"

"You have the whole place to yourself, sir. Their excellencies prefer to stay in town, at the Justice Ministry's rest house. That's where all the restaurants and life is. Not enough people around here. Nobody's stayed here for more than a week in over twenty years. The last one who lasted his full period of service here was Counsellor Hanna Fayez. He's related to you, sir, right?"

"No. He's not. I've never heard of him."

"Anyway, nobody lasts more than a week in this place. After that, they move into the judge's rest house in the district capital."

Having made that point a second time, he gave me a mischievous smile that matched his countenance.

"And why's that?"

Forcing himself to look serious, he said, "The people around here think this lodge is haunted. They hear voices at night ever since the original owner, a foreigner, was murdered here."

He paused to gauge my reaction. I kept my face blank.

"You know what? You'd be doing the Justice Ministry a favor if you told them to sell this place. They'll have no trouble finding a buyer."

He paused, then muttered beneath his breath, though loud enough for me to hear, "A couple of days, and you'll be joining the others."

2

MY MOTHER WAS LIVID. SHE spat a stream of curses at me, then turned back to the wall and gasped for a second time. Head cocked to the side, she squinted at what I'd written and tried to mouth the letters, but failed. She slapped her chest with the palm of her hand, ran her fingers over the lines, then recoiled. She flicked off a sandal, snatched it up, and readied for the attack. My father appeared just in time to spare me the thrashing. As he came over and gently took me into his embrace, her bared teeth recoiled, and she backed away. The danger had passed. She merely took another mournful look at the wall and said, "Have you no shame, you little she-devil? We just had the house painted."

"Those are God's words," said my father, pointing to handiwork. He always stood up for me.

My mother's shoulders slumped. "Well, then, as long as those are God's words, I suppose it's OK," she muttered before going back into the kitchen to finish cooking. She combined lunch and dinner into a single daily meal, which my father ate with us when he returned from the field at sunset.

My father was as illiterate as she was. How did that escape her? Maybe she didn't want to embarrass him. He was as hard on her as he was soft toward me. The storm had abated, but the incident would stay lodged in my memory along with many others that would happen soon.

I went to my room, still thinking about the sentence that I'd etched on the wall with a nail. I'd learned it in school that day, and it puzzled me:

"Though God does not answer all our prayers, He fulfills all His promises."

How often I prayed to Him to free me from my mother's torments. But it was my father who departed from this world first, and far too soon.

Ten years flew by like a high speed train, too fast to count the cars on the way, let alone make out the passengers. It was impossible to forget what my mother did to me, though, and the stables, where I stood, brought all the painful memories back to life. That place embodied them like a snake that strikes over and over from the same lair.

Nothing bound me to my home. I had lost my compass; I had been patient when I should have cried, and the reverse. My mother's second husband took away my hope of remaining a virgin until I married. He assaulted me while I was asleep, when no one else was home. He tore off my nightgown and yanked my panties down. I didn't dare resist. I was so weak back then, submissive, fragile—like leaves that scatter from their branches at the first gust of an autumn wind. Later, I learned he had put a mild drug in my food. It kept me awake, but numbed my will.

If my girlhood died that day, my husband Khidr took care of its burial soon after. Not that I had been entirely naive or innocent. Ever since I was a child, I grasped at the illusion of freedom. I imagined it, dreamed it, but I never slept deeply enough to really experience my dream. I was like Khidr in this respect. We were both waiting for something that could never happen, and deep down we both knew it.

He was too jealous to leave me in the house alone and insisted I accompany him to the stables. There, my whole life story was laid bare before me, retold through the most important chapters, exposed in the most brutal scenes, digging deeper and more painful grooves in my heart.

"Come on, boy!" shouted the handler for the third time. I could see him clearly from where I stood. His feet sank deeper into the mud and dung as he pushed the stallion from behind. Khidr clamped the tail of his galabiya between his teeth and pushed too. They sweated and grunted as they coaxed the horse into mating with a nervous mare. She stood, tall and proud, in a darkened corner of the stable. Somehow she had resigned herself to that miserable excuse for a stallion. This was the third time they failed to get the aging male to mount her. He was probably sterile. That's what the handler thought. But my husband defended the poor thing, even as he continued to beat it.

"Mount, you son of a bitch! Mount!"

Spittle sprayed from his mouth as he swore and lashed the rump of the horse with a crop. At last, the horse managed to mount, but gave up after only a few seconds. The mare took a couple of hesitant steps forward, turning her head back slightly to give the horse a worried glance. She seemed to be making up her mind whether or not to encourage him to try again. The old male looked down with watery eyes. Time and age had taken their toll. His arousal flagged. Apparently, those days were over.

Khidr refused to give up. He called for the handler to help, but he was exhausted and plopped down on the ground to rest his back and head against the stall wall.

"Come on, get up," Khidr said.

By way of an answer, the handler leaned his body to one side and released a loud fart. With a flick of the arm, he then dismissed Khidr and the horses, closed his eyes, and fell asleep.

Khidr was nothing if not stubborn. He started pushing again, glaring at me to get up and help. My whole body trembled under that scowl. I feared he had caught a glimmer in my eyes when he failed. Was I going to laugh or cry? In both cases, my mouth always broadened, my eyes narrowed, and a noise escaped my throat. In both cases, the lump back there was always bitter. On that occasion, I clamped my mouth closed and smiled. But no matter how hard I tried to hold back, a laugh escaped me.

"How dare you laugh at me, you whore!" He looked around for something to throw at me, but I was a step ahead of him. I grabbed a rock and threw it at the impotent horse, which caused it to whinny and rear up.

Khidr's eyes bulged like a madman and his nose flared. He could smell my fear. He picked up his shoe and charged. I ran toward the house. I made it inside ahead of him, but he caught up with me before I could hide behind the oven. He snatched my head covering, yanked me to him, and threw me to the ground. I covered my face to keep his huge hands from pummeling it. He kicked me in my belly, while I curled up like a fetus. I tried to suppress my groans. I had learned from experience that the louder I cried, the fiercer he got.

Suddenly he stopped and the room fell silent. I heard some rustling and clinking sounds nearby. I cracked upon an eye to see what he was up to. He was searching for something in the large wicker hamper. I gasped. In a second he would find the branding iron. He'd heat it up and use it to burn me like he did last year and the year before when he found out I had lied about being pregnant. He refused to believe that he was sterile. He was convinced that I was to blame. I tried to hide among the clutter in the room, but Khidr's large body, as thick as a brick wall, blocked all paths to safety. He stood by the oven, heating up the branding iron, muttering, threatening. I'd jinxed the mare because I was barren. He was going to teach me a lesson.

The heavy mill handle was within reach. I plucked up my courage and silently shifted my weight. I leapt, grabbed hold of the handle with both hands, and smashed it down on Khidr's skull.

I stood transfixed by the blood gushing out of him. He froze like a statue, mouth agape, then his eyeballs rolled upward into his head, and he toppled to the floor with a loud moan. The branding iron seared his belly and his thighs, and soon he was screaming in pain. His body jerked violently for several seconds, then fell still. He was dead.

I stared at the prone corpse, my knees trembling. The horror of what happened crawled beneath my skin like armies of ants. I had just killed my husband. I hadn't meant to. The next thing I knew, I was running through the fields, crying so hard the front of my galabiya was soaked in tears. My vision was blurred. I rubbed my eyes so hard, I nearly dislodged them from their sockets. I came to an intersection. Should I head to the train station or flag down a taxi? As I wavered between these two options, I forgot the more important question: where to?

3

I PRETENDED NOT TO HAVE heard Ramses's remark about my being unable to last a week here. As I continued to inspect the judges' lodge, arms folded behind my back, I recounted to him what I had learned about the place. It was my answer to that look on his face that said I had no clue as to what to expect.

The lodge was originally constructed for a British irrigation engineer who was in charge of northern Upper Egypt. He lived here for years until they found his murdered body in the front yard. That was in the early 1940s, a few years after King Farouk ascended the throne. It was reported that he was shot soon after a quarrel with a local farmer called Abdallah. Yet investigators found that this Abdallah was nowhere near the lodge at the time. He'd spent that whole day at a coffee-house and, naturally, there were dozens of people to testify to this. So the prosecution attributed the murder to "unidentified assailants" and the case went cold.

"But the British didn't let it end there," Ramses broke in with the eagerness of someone who knows the end of the story.

"Hold your horses. I'm getting there," I said and went on to recount how the British, infuriated by the prosecution's decision to drop the case, took matters into their own hands.

"They avenged the civil engineer by exacting retribution from all the farmers in the village. Before long, their fields went dry and their crops withered and died. There were also stories about how the son of that Englishman fell in love with a beautiful peasant girl called Nour. His infatuation with her also died, but by then the damage was done."

Ramses nodded.

"Over time, the village became predominantly Coptic. They migrated up here from the south, replacing the Muslims who had migrated to the Delta. That's when the people started to call the village Abu Saliba. Afterwards—"

Ramses interrupted me again, "That would be after my grandfather on my mother's side. His name was Salib. He moved here from Assiut and taught these people how to weave Bedouin rugs. Before long, this place became the most famous carpet producing village in the whole country. But talk about ingratitude. Instead of honoring him, they poked fun at his name."

I doubted that the drug, some kind of Valium substitute, commonly referred to as Abu Saliba because of the X etched on the back of the pill, existed in Ramses' father's time, let alone his grandfather's. In fact, I doubted people had his grandfather in mind at all when they nicknamed the village, even if *Salib* is another word for cross. Most likely, the name was inspired by the village's cross-topped spires, which would have been seen for miles, distinguishing it and its inhabitants from the Muslim-majority villages in Upper Egypt. Noticing his scowl, I mentioned none of this, and instead invited him to sit with me and tell me about the people here and the ways of life in the village. It was a way to pass the time. Nights here promised to be long and dreary and the days too short. As it turned out, I did most of the talking.

I resumed my account, skipping ahead to the post-1952 Egyptian revolution, when they renamed the village Tayea, after the village mayor at the time, Mohammed Tayea. Even then, the villagers insisted on mispronouncing the name. They called it *Tayha*, as in "the lost soul" instead of "the obedient one." That was done to spite the mayor's family. Evidently, this Mohammed Tayea was a staunch supporter of the revolution, despite the harm it caused the Coptic landowners. Quite a few of them were arrested, thrown into jail, and dispossessed of their properties within the first two years of the revolution. One story has it that the mayor slaughtered two large calves which he'd named King Farouk and King Fouad, in honor of President Gamal Abdel Nasser and other members of the Revolutionary Command Council during a visit to the village. They appointed Tayea mayor for life as a result, and the title became hereditary. It's been passed down from father to son up to the present day.

Ramses rolled his eyes. "Yeah. And they took afternoon tea in his home and spent the night there too because he swore up and down he'd divorce his wife if they refused. The next day, he waved them goodbye as they drove off with gift-wrapped packages of homemade fermented cheese and mud-oven baked pastries."

Ramses's voice dripped with sarcasm. Evidently, he wasn't impressed with my history of the rest house. I laughed and said, "But seriously, Ramses. Is it the whole story you don't believe? Or is it just the bit about the calves and Abdel Nasser's visit?"

"They're just stories, sir. About the Tayea family and this place. And there are tons of more stories. They've been going around for ages and no one knows where they came from. Folks here call a lie a lie and believe it at the same time."

He paused as though to swallow something bitter.

"It was Nour, the mayor's daughter, who set off the whole train of disasters in the village long ago when she took off like a flaming dove and vanished. No one heard from her again. That's probably why we've called the village, Tayha, the lost one. But, as I said, these are all stories. Tayea, Tayha, what's the difference? Neither controls their own fate."

He scratched the back of his head then asked timidly, "What's your full name, sir? The message from the courthouse notifying me of your arrival only mentioned your first and second name."

"Why do you want to know?"

He paused, confused, but only for a split second.

"So I can procure the food supplies for the rest house in your name, sir. We're men of the law, sir. We're not going to break it, are we?"

"My name is Nader Fayez Kamal. Put all the household expenses on my account. I want to make sure they get deducted from my salary. That is if we want to abide by the law, as you say."

"You're from Assiut, sir. Right?"

I gave him a noncommittal smile as I pulled out my wallet and handed him a hundred-pound bill to cover the weekly household expenses. I told him I took breakfast at eight in the morning and listed the kinds of food I like. He handed me two keys, one for the front door, the other for the back, then left. I watched him as he headed off toward one of the two outbuildings while singing a strange folk song I'd never heard before:

"Mohammed Ali's tree grew too tall, Gamal cut it down.
I once walked with my head bowed, Gamal lifted it up.
The good days have come. Good night Gamal"

My cell phone pierced the silence as he disappeared into the darkness. It was my fiancée, Farida, wanting to make sure I'd arrived safely and to reproach me for having had my phone turned off. Her words poured out of the receiver like machine gunfire and quickly gave me a headache. I could not get a word in edgewise. I tried to tell her that I hadn't turned off my phone, that the signal was probably weak down here. She was never a good listener. It took several repetitions before she said in an irritated voice, "Well, why didn't you say so to begin with instead of letting me get all worked up and worried about you!"

Her tone softened as she turned to other matters. She reminded me to keep checking for available plots of land allocated for Ministry of Justice employees in the new satellite cities around Cairo. I was to reserve one or two in our name so that we could take advantage of the discount. "Then we can sell them off later when the prices go up. Or better yet, we could sell one plot and build a small villa on the other."

"Yes, dear . . . I will, dear . . ." I said, dutifully saying whatever would be necessary to end that discussion. But it was like trying to douse a fire that wouldn't go out.

When at last I managed to change the subject, I told her about my new accommodation. I described the idyllic scenery, the tranquility, and the keeper, Ramses. I could hear her stifling a yawn, but she brightened up when the conversation turned back to perks and property. Her sister's husband, a police academy graduate, had worked as a public prosecutor for a short period, but didn't like the job. For the hundredth time, she reminded me how Magdi had resigned from the prosecutor's office in order to become a counselor for the State Litigation Authority. Yet again, she enumerated the many benefits he received just for being assigned as counsel to four ministries at once. I could rattle them off by rote before they were even out of her mouth: "Two cars plus driver from two ministries, a car for the family from another, and four retainer allowances, each as much as his basic salary. And don't forget the ministers he's gotten to know, especially the Minister of Housing . . ."

All attempts to change the subject were futile, including interrupting and speaking over her. I hung up and continued to ignore her calls until the phone fell silent. Sometimes, this abrupt method was the only one that worked. The following morning, I would send her a saved SMS with all I needed to say, so she would read without interrupting. Then I would call:

"My dearest, my cell phone battery died. I'm so sorry to have missed the rest of our conversation."

I'd wait for her to read and call her up to apologize, after which all would be forgotten.

I glanced at my wristwatch. The hands were about to embrace in celebration of the advent of a new day. I yawned. It was time to turn in. It being autumn, I'd chosen a bedroom facing south, sunnier and away from the prevailing wind. Just as I was about to take off my tie, someone knocked at the front door. The knocking grew more persistent and so forceful that I feared one of the double panels would fly off its hinges.

The colleague whom I'd replaced had told me to bring my gun with me. My alarm and confusion mounted as the pounding grew louder and faster. I reached to my left side, took hold of my gun, then remembered the chamber was empty.

4

I RACED THROUGH THE FIELDS until I reached the train station. I stopped to catch my breath. My ribs felt like they were about to burst through my chest. Reaching into my galabiya, I pulled out my small money bag and headed to the ticket window. I was nervous, confused, looking behind me every other second.

"Where to?" The man in the ticket booth asked, snatching the bill from my hand without looking up. His fingers hovered over the receipt books waiting for my answer. Just then, a newsboy passed by, shouting out the headlines. I didn't catch much, but it was enough to solve my dilemma.

"Beni Soueif," I said in a low, timid voice.

I found a seat in a second-class carriage near an open door. A few men of various ages were gathered there to smoke and chat. They practically had to shout in order to make themselves heard over the clacking of the train's wheels on the tracks. I pressed my eyes shut to keep from crying. The noise pounded on the inside of my skull as the train sped forward, trampling everything in its path, just like Khidr trampled several years of my life. The "late Khidr," I muttered to myself.

I prayed silently, begging the Lord to guard my secret and protect me. About half an hour after I boarded the train, my head began to droop to my chest. I tightened the knot of my headscarf on my forehead as a way to force myself to stay awake. Suddenly the train sounded its whistle and slowed to a stop. As it sat there, I began to feel restless and in need of some air. I got up and, moving calmly, I went to the open door where the men politely moved apart to give me a little space. I breathed deeply, greedily, filling my lungs with fresh air, but my hands were still trembling. I turned at a sudden commotion coming from inside my carriage. A police officer in his khaki uniform was moving up the aisle. He was followed by a sergeant with a large pot belly hanging over his belt and a conscript as skinny as a pencil. They were asking the passengers for their IDs. They were only a couple of rows away. A glint in the officer's eyes told me he could smell my fear. He looked ready to skip the few rows between us to nab me.

Did I really hear someone say they were hunting for Khidr's killer, or did I just imagine it? My brain must have stopped thinking, because without knowing it, I leapt to the door, jumped off the train, and took to my heels. The men at the door had probably frozen mid-puff, gaping at my back. I didn't turn around to look. I didn't pause for a second, even when one of them yelled, "Come back, lady. There are jackals out there!"

I tore through field after field. I leapt across a narrow ditch and came to a small pool of stagnant water. I judged the distance wrong. My left foot slipped, I teetered backward and ended up in the muck. I wrung out the tail of my galabiya and shook the fabric to dry it, but it was no use. It was completely soiled. After a short while, it began to give off a rotten odor that would not go away no matter how much I tried to rub off the mud.

My bare feet were killing me, but I kept walking. At last I saw a small mosque. It wasn't lit, but I noticed a faint light coming from the building next to it.

"Hail Mary, full of grace!" I almost shouted before bursting into tears. I continued to pray as I headed toward that light, reciting, "Then call and I will answer, or let me speak, and Thou answer me." Suddenly, a sheikh in a turban appeared in front of me in the dark.

"Who are you? What are you doing here at this time of night?"

I stood with my mouth open, unable to respond. I glanced at the window with the light, and said, "Nour. My name's Nour."

"Nour? Dear Lord." He took a step back. "By Your hidden grace, deliver us from what we fear. Spare us from Your wrath and fury. Do you have an ID?"

My stomach sank. The name I chose meant "light," but it seemed to have upset the sheikh. I said the first thing that came to mind. "It was stolen earlier—my ID. I'm a stranger here. I'm—"

"We're all strangers to this world. What's your father's name? Where do you come from?"

"Nour Rizq. I'm from Assiut. My father was the mayor there, but he died a long time ago. I was visiting some of my relatives here. But I lost track of time and missed the train. I just want to spend the night here in the mosque. I'll leave first thing at dawn."

"This here's a guesthouse and activities center, not a mosque. Now pray to the Prophet, my dear. Take a breath and tell us your story from the beginning."

My whole body trembled. "Praise be to the Prophet. May peace be upon him," I said, willing the words out of my mouth as my mind begged the Holy Virgin to save me. His eyes seemed to bore right through me as though to expose the lies and confirm his suspicions about me. I could tell by his frown that he didn't believe my story or that I was lost, even though I truly was. But in the end he agreed, grudgingly, to let me stay in the guesthouse. Maybe he was so irritated by my weeping and sniffling that he decided to buy himself some peace of mind until the morning. He studied me silently, clicking impatiently through his prayer beads with that frown still on his face. "God forgive us," he muttered several times below his breath. Then out loud, he said, "I want you out of here at the crack of dawn."

I nodded my agreement. His eyes shifted toward my hands. I held the hem of my sleeve with my fingers so it wouldn't slip up and reveal the cross tattooed on the inside of my wrist. Once inside, he called for the caretaker who appeared from an inner room. The sheikh whispered something in his ear that I couldn't make out.

They gave me an upstairs room. From the window, I heard the caretaker bid farewell to the sheikh, whom he called Sheikh Ragab. I watched the old man pick his way down the path, using the light from his cell phone, until he was swallowed up by darkness. I sighed, wiped the tears from my eyes, and thanked the Blessed Virgin for having come to my aid. As I moved away from the window, a heavy hand tapped my shoulder. I jumped and spun around. It was the caretaker, bearing an idiotic grin that revealed two rows of crooked, tobacco-stained teeth. I stepped away from him. He laughed, his eyes fixed on my breasts as he set a thin woolen blanket on the mattress.

"So where in Assiut are you from, sweetheart? I bet you're from El Badari. It's famous for its pretty girls."

He sat down on the edge of the bed, fished into his pocket, and pulled out a matchbox to light a cigarette. I groaned inwardly. This was going to last longer than one cigarette.

All the names of the Assiut towns I knew escaped me. If I tried to play along, he'd call me out in no time.

"Actually, I should tell you, my mother's from here," I said, sneaking a glance at the window. "That's who I was visiting. But I had a spat with her husband, so I'm going back to my husband and children in Assiut in the morning."

There was a long silence as he sat studying me. He pulled out another cigarette, then just as he was about to stick it in his mouth, he said,

"How about a cup of tea?"

"No. Thanks. I'm really tired. I just want to sleep."

"Your mother—Is her name Dumyana, and does she live just to the west of the market?"

I was so taken aback by the question that I pointed in a different direction and said, "No, her name's Hoda and she lives to the north, near the irrigation canal."

The servant's eyebrows knitted in confusion. His mouth twisted into a sneer as he stared at my body up and down. He started to fish for something between his teeth with his fingernail. After a moment, he found what he was looking for, rolled it between his fingers and flicked it toward a corner of the room.

"So that makes you a neighbor of Father Samuel."

I hesitated, but then he gave me an encouraging smile, and I nodded. His smile broadened and he snapped it shut. He handed me the key to the room and left without saying another word.

I was just about to fall asleep when I heard him knock on the door.

"What is it?" I asked without opening the door.

"Sheikh Ragab told me to take care of you. So I made you a cup of tea. The sugar's on the side, because you're sweet enough already. And there's a tasty savory pastry here and some soft cheese waiting for you. I bet you're starving. The tray's outside your door. I'm leaving now. Good night."

I heard a door open and shut slowly and the sound of his feet moving away.

I couldn't get to sleep. For the next hour or so, I tossed and turned. I thought I imagined two men whispering outside my door. I slipped out of bed and crept to the door as stealthily as a cat. I heard the caretaker tell the other person that he'd slipped a sedative into my tea and that he had a second key to my room. In a few more minutes, an hour would be up, and he'd sneak into my room.

"I'm sorry, Saleh, but if Sheikh Ragab finds out that you took the spare key from me, you'll be in a lot of trouble and I'm not going to help you."

"So what if he finds out? I've got my answer ready. I'll just repeat back to him what he tells us, line and verse. Isn't he one who goes on night and day about how Copts are heretics and idolaters, which makes it alright for us to take their women? Isn't he the one who says it's sinful for us to wish them well on their holidays and who has us recite curses against them during Friday prayers? Don't look at me that way. Egypt's not going to suffer if I fuck that lying Christian bitch. I'm not the problem here."

"Come on, Saleh. The poor girl must have really had a rough time, so she came here for help. Just let her be, for God's sake. Stop being an asshole."

The guy's voice was trembling with emotion, but Saleh had the devil in him.

"You're so naive. I told you, I saw the cross on her wrist. I'll give my right arm if she isn't on the run from her husband who caught her in bed with her lover. Now get out of my head and stop spoiling my mood. All you have to do is mind the front door. I'm not going to tell anyone you were in on this. Look, you've got five pounds in your pocket. So what do you say?"

The guy paused, then said, "I say thanks for the five pounds and Saleh who?"

I silently slapped my cheeks as tears sprung to my eyes. Looking desperately around the room, I caught sight of the tray with the tea and the food he'd left me. Thank God I hadn't touched it. I heard footsteps walking away and floorboards creaking outside my room. I could hear his breathing grow louder and heavier. I heard the key fumbling, fitting into the keyhole, preparing to turn the latch.

I pressed my eyes shut. Crossing myself, I whispered beneath my breath, "Help me, Holy Mother of God. I fly unto you. Hear me, answer me!"

I tiptoed toward the window as quietly as I could. I heard a strange noise on the other side, low and rumbling. I peered out, but couldn't see anything. The sound was terrifying.

5

I PEEKED DOWN FROM MY bedroom window, thinking that perhaps my mind was playing tricks on me. I was startled by what I saw. No less than twenty villagers were out front, holding kerosene lamps and torches with flickering flames. Some of the men were grumbling, but I couldn't make out what they said. Their leader had to be the one in the middle, because the rest kept a respectful distance—enough for him to adjust his abaya from time to time, or to spread his arms, if he wanted. The fists kept pounding on the door, so hard I thought they would knock it down. I raced down the wooden stairs and flung open the door with a scowl to emphasize my irritation. The crowd was even larger than I had thought. The leader, a distinguished-looking elderly man with graying hair and a thin moustache, raised his hands high in the air. The men fell silent.

"I'm Judge Radwan, son," he said with a confident smile, "May we come in?"

I caught sight of Ramses squeezing his way forward through the crowd. Our eyes met. He shot me a warning look, which I wasn't sure how to read. I stood aside.

"Please come in. But I'm afraid there aren't enough chairs for all your guests, sir."

He laughed as he stepped inside and the rest followed like a human deluge, filling the living room in seconds.

"Obviously you're new to Upper Egypt, sir. There's plenty of room on the floor. We'll make ourselves at home."

He went over to the couch and took a seat in the middle. The rest of the men squatted on their haunches around us, with one exception: a tall, burly guy who took up a position behind the judge, meaty hands resting on a cane as thick as the features of his face. Ramses stood behind me, proud, shoulders squared as though he'd appointed himself my guardian angel.

"We haven't had the honor yet, Nader Bey. Um, I never did catch your full name."

I turned to Ramses with a smile. At least he had been a little bit more subtle when fishing for my religious affiliation. He answered on my behalf, pointedly enunciating each syllable:

"This is Nader Fayez Bey. He's from Assiut too."

That last bit Ramses volunteered from his imagination. I let it pass, just as he had passed over my last name, which comes from my grandfather. Rectifying the disinformation could wait until after I found out what this man's problem was.

Addressing me with the familiarity of someone who had known me for years, Judge Radwan inquired in a general way about my work with the Public Prosecutor's Office. One might have thought him a senior supervisor asking an underling for a report. Sometimes, he took my answers as an excuse to digress on judiciary affairs with what, to me, seemed an unwarranted air of self-importance. Yet, his repeated failures to correct various erroneous details that I deliberately slipped into my answers caused my suspicions to grow until I felt compelled to interrupt him politely.

"Excuse me sir, which circuit did you say you're currently assigned to?"

"I've retired," he answered curtly.

He started to broach the subject he had come to discuss, but I interrupted him again.

"What was the last court you worked with?"

Quickly surveying the men around him, he lowered his voice to say, "My dear son, I'm not with the judiciary. I was a counsellor-at-law for the Wastewater Authority."

"Well, why didn't you say so from the start? An attorney for the government. That's great. So, you and your men must be here to sequester the Ministry of Justice rest house. Am I right, Radwan?"

Ramses was the only one to laugh at my joke. Everyone else glared at me with looks darker than the pitch black night outside. The "judge" narrowed his eyes at me. I had wounded his pride by stripping him of the honorifics and addressing him by his first name. Leaning back in his seat and crossing his legs in an attempt to regain his standing, he said, "I want my rights and the rights of my people. I want my land and my fields. I want to safeguard my rights against the Bishoi clan, Nader Bey."

"Okay. I'll see what I can do. Why don't you drop by my office tomorrow morning, sir, and we'll discuss it then."

"Tomorrow morning? We're going to wait until sunup so we can fill out a bunch of paperwork? Hell no. You're the Office of Prosecution here. I swear by God Almighty, I'm not budging from this place unless you come with me right now to do a boundary inspection on a plot of land that's rightfully mine and issue a ruling in my favor."

I turned to Ramses and held his gaze in search of a clue. His sullen expression practically mouthed the word, "No."

I remained seated and relaxed, as though I hadn't heard Radwan's ultimatum. He was now engaged in a whispered conversation on his cell phone, which he had extracted from the folds of his abaya. My confusion must have gotten the better of my attempt at cool silence and showed on my face, judging from some of the knowing looks and exchanges among the men around me. Suddenly, the rest house's land-line rang, saving me by the bell. Ramses hastened to answer, then held the receiver toward me and announced as solemnly as a bailiff:

"His Excellency, the District Public Prosecutor, Mahmoud Hassan Bey, is on the phone, Nader Bey."

The room fell silent in deference to the venerable presence of my new boss, even if through the medium of a phone line. Mahmoud Bey's voice sounded friendly. He gave me a warm welcome and arranged a time for me to drop by his office the following day to meet him. I tried to interrupt him in order to explain my predicament, but he wouldn't give me an opening. Then, just as I thought he was about to end the conversation, he said, "Judge Radwan is with you right now, I know. You see, he's one of the local dignitaries, and things here in the district work differently to what you're familiar with in Cairo. Go with them and do the survey, issue a provisional usufruct grant, and give him a copy. But don't say a word of this to the Bishois. I'll explain everything to you tomorrow."

"But sir, it's late. And it's not like this is a murder requiring an inspection of the crime scene or—"

The district prosecutor's tone shifted abruptly from affable to peremptory.

"This is the job, Nader Bey. You don't get to pick and choose. This is an official call. Enter it in your report. Oh, and from now on, get used to keeping your cell phone switched on, especially at night. Goodbye."

I replaced the receiver. Radwan muttered some words of gratitude into his cell phone, and hung up. So this was a three-way call.

Ramses lowered his eyes and bowed his head. The old man was seasoned in the ways here. He must have guessed what Mahmoud Bey had told me. After a moment's silence, he moved listlessly toward the door, as though hoping I'd call him back.

"Should I get the car ready and call the clerk at the office, sir?" he asked.

"Yes." He sounded so hopeless that I couldn't bring myself to say a word more.

Radwan stood up and, on cue, his men got up and huddled around him, awaiting orders. With a triumphant smile, he came up to me, put his hand on my shoulder and said, "I'll be waiting in my car, son. You can follow in yours. I'll show you the way because you're new to these parts."

After a half hour drive on a wide unpaved road, we arrived at a large expanse of fields. The moon was moving into a partial eclipse that night, so visibility was poor. The heavens were probably angry at what we were about to do. I set to work with the aid of the kerosene lamps and the torches of Radwan's men. Radwan had handed me an old cadastral map that I could barely make out beneath the flickering flames. It was not easy to determine whether or not the border posts had been moved. I doubted that Radwan had a rightful claim, despite the government eagle seal that graced a corner of the map, and the dozens of ornate signatures from directors of agricultural units, Ministry of Agriculture deputy ministers, and secretary generals. The villagers preserved an expectant silence, broken only by mutterings that urged me to be patient and keep going whenever they sensed my frustration. How could they read me so easily? Suddenly I had an idea that sat well with my conscience.

"Get me the local surveyor."

"But he's asleep now," someone volunteered.

I smiled to myself. My way out lay open before me. I collected my papers, rolled up the map, straightened my back, and turned to leave. My relief, though, was short-lived.

"Hold on," Radwan said, "the surveyor lives close by." Turning to one of his men, he ordered, "Go fetch Awad, even if you have to drag him here in his nightshirt."

While we waited, some bright lights suddenly flashed from a tower in the distance. Noticing my surprise, Radwan explained, "That big thing's a church, sir. Imagine that. And there are three more of them in the village, and just one solitary mosque. We're surrounded, sir. It's like a siege, by God."

He snapped his mouth shut and looked at me uncomfortably. I kept my face blank and said nothing to confirm or deny his sudden suspicion.

"True, they are all houses of the Lord," he said, recalibrating his approach "and those people, they're our brothers. But justice is a good thing too, isn't it, sir? I mean, it's just not right for a church to swallow up a mosque."

I ignored him, and went back to work as soon as the surveyor arrived. The man, Awad, had been thoroughly coached. His abaya ballooned out over an immense potbelly, creating a tent of fabric big enough to hide one of Radwan's minions. Whenever I asked Awad a question, he read his answer from Radwan, whose eyes were his teleprompter.

After I completed the inspection, I asked a few more routine questions. I scribbled my ruling on a scrap of paper and handed it to the clerk with instructions to enter it in the books in a legible script and not to divulge it to either party. I then gave Radwan a perfunctory handshake and headed to the courthouse car. He did not even bother to conceal his triumphant smile. I kept mine to myself.

Back at the courthouse lodge, I let the hot shower gush over my head and shoulders, closing my eyes as my muscles relaxed and my aches were washed away. It felt that I'd had dirt and bugs clinging to my skin and now I was that much lighter.

I tucked myself beneath the heavy blankets and fell into a deep sleep. The image of Radwan followed me across the threshold of unconsciousness into my dreams. He had taken the form of a huge bird with black wings, circling over the rest house. His screeching caws pursued me. If I fled to one room and shut the door, I'd hear him outside the window. If I fled to another, he'd follow. Then Ramses appeared holding a tiny rifle, too small to scare a fly, though as soon as he pulled the trigger, it made a boom loud enough to make a lion cower in his lair. Radwan plummeted to the ground, the large black feathers of his wings scattered in the air. One of them settled on my face, covering it so completely, the world turned black.

6

MY MIND ORDERED MY LEGS to move, and they obeyed instantly, as though they had been waiting for this command. I leaped from the window, which must have been three yards from the ground. When I stood up—unhurt, miraculously—I found myself staring at a dog. All I could make out was his huge maw and the intense gleam in his eyes. The rest of it took its color from the pitch black night. Its rumbling growl grew into a frightening snarl. It approached warily at first, the drool dripping from its bared teeth. It barked rapidly like a machine gun and pounced. It only just missed my flesh because it was tied up, but it managed to clench the hem of my galabiya. I wrenched it free from its powerful jaws and ran. In seconds, it slipped its leash and started to chase me. I was barely inches ahead of it when I leapt over a dead palm trunk that lay across the path. The dog stopped right there, as though that was its boundary. Maybe it was actually trying to help me. As my father always said, trust the dog, not his owner.

I ducked into the cornfields where the cloak of night was thicker, and kept running. I heard Saleh shouting, "Nour!" and the dog barking, but I paid them no mind. Soon, I began to feel dizzy, strained by my nerves and my despair. I sat down on the ground before my legs gave out, and wept.

After some moments, I collected myself and looked around. I spotted a sign on my right, but it was too dark to make out what it said. Beyond that, I saw what appeared to be a villa partly hidden behind a clump of trees. The light from the windows flickered through the branches. Somebody was still up at that time. I quickly pushed through the shrubbery until I reached a back door and knocked. A gray-haired man opened it with a startled expression and stared at me without uttering a word. I saw a cross tattooed on the wrist of the hand he used to hold up his lantern. I let out a deep sigh and smiled with relief. He brought his arm down quickly as I collapsed at his feet, the smile still on my lips.

The man slapped my face a few times as gently as he could. He must have thought I'd fainted. I lifted a finger to let him know I was still conscious. I simply couldn't get up when he urged me to. He tried to lift me up, but he wasn't strong enough. Eventually, by pulling me beneath the arms he managed to bring me into the living room. As he sat me on a chair, he noticed the cross on my wrist and smiled.

"My name's Ramses Iskander. This here's the courthouse lodge, and I'm the caretaker. What's your name, dear? Where have you come from?"

"Please, sir, let me stay here until the morning. I beg you. I'm a stranger here and the people in the mosque kicked me out and—"

He put a finger to his lips to silence me.

"Don't worry. You'll be safe here."

But the warmth had gone out of his voice even as he tried to reassure me. It was as though his smile had taken flight at the word "mosque." He closed the front door, gave the key a turn in the lock, and put it in his pocket. Then he turned to go upstairs, signaling me to follow. My stomach began to knot all over again. I fought against the fear that he might hurt me, and followed cautiously. He paused in front of a door and knocked a couple of times. Without waiting for an answer, he then turned the knob softly, stepped into the room, and flicked on the light. My curiosity forced me to follow.

A young man was asleep in his bed. He rolled over lazily, yawned and cracked open half an eye. Suddenly, he bolted upright, reached under his pillow and pulled out a gun.

"It's me, Ramses! By the living Christ, I'm the caretaker, Ramses."

The old man said nothing more as the young gentleman stared at him, then his widened eyes turned to me. His mouth seemed to move, as though struggling for words. He lowered the gun and, with his other hand, he dismissed us, saying he would join us in a minute downstairs.

That was how I met Deputy Public Prosecutor Nader Fayez. While we waited downstairs, Ramses told me he had just arrived in Tayea less than a day earlier.

"He's a good Christian. He's from Cairo, but he comes from a prominent family in Assiut."

So he's an outsider in this village like me, I thought. I felt a kind of kinship with him and thought that was why I had felt comforted by his soft voice, despite the gun he had pointed at us. As they say, people thrown into similar circumstances grow close quickly. According to Ramses, he was about five years younger than me. He must have had some heavy troubles weighing on him, because he looked much older. Ramses also told me that Nader Bey had only just returned from some official duty. That would explain why he looked so haggard as he descended the wooden stairs. He was tall, brown-skinned, and had jet black hair which he had neatly combed. He frowned as though he had found himself in a bad dream that tied his tongue.

"I'm Hoda Yusef Habib," I said, handing him my ID card.

He yawned a few times, although that could have been to conceal his irritation at being woken and having to deal with this awkward situation. At last he said, "What brings you here in the middle of the night, Hoda? Who are you running from and why?"

I told him my story, except for the part where I killed my husband in self-defense and fled. I also left out the fact that Khidr was Muslim, and I added a minor detail I felt was necessary.

"I lost my husband in Iraq many years ago. I haven't remarried," I said in the matter-of-fact voice of a widow long accustomed to her bereavement.

"And what are you running from?"

Nader Bey had adopted the probing tone of an investigator. He looked unconvinced, as though trying to separate the wheat of my story from the chaff.

Thinking quickly, I said, "My mother's husband attacked me. I ran away, not knowing where I was going, until I found myself at the train station. I got on a train and off in this village, thinking it was Beni Soueif, my late father's hometown."

He fixed his eyes on mine without saying a word. His mind was turning over my last addition, examining it for holes. I could tell he found something when a gleam came into his eyes and he irritably lit a cigarette. Before he could ask me more questions, I swore I was telling the truth, repeated some of the more painful parts, and broke down in tears. The tears were genuine. They gushed down my cheeks and I couldn't turn off the faucet. To my surprise, Ramses backed me up. Nader shook his head rapidly several times, as though refusing to let my fiction take hold, then turned to Ramses who was grinning for some reason.

"With your permission, sir," he said before Nader could speak, "let me take her to the church in the morning. Father Stephanos will take care of her and protect her until she can return to her village. No offence, sir, but the government in these parts isn't going to stand up for one of us. Or do you advise us to file a complaint against Sheikh Ragab and that servant of his?"

Nader Bey seemed to grimace in answer to that question, then he yawned and stood up.

"Okay. But she can't stay here. Make her some tea and give her some breakfast. It's only a couple more hours until sunup. Take her to the church then. As for filing a complaint, that's for her to decide."

Ramses led me to a small cabin next to the rest house, which was where he lived. Once inside, he locked the door and went over to the small window and pulled the curtains shut. He then prepared some tea and put some biscuits filled with date paste on a plate.

"Are you fasting?"

I shook my head. He set the plate before me and watched me as I ate hungrily. As soon as I finished one biscuit, he would gesture for me to take another, which I did until I had my fill. I thanked him for his kindness and hospitality. He smiled, but it was not a warm smile.

"So what are your plans? I'm not a public prosecutor or a police officer. I'm a Copt like you. Tell me God's honest truth, so I can help you. Do you really want to go back to your village? Or is it that you have nobody to go back to and you want to stay here and live with us?

Despite that smile which made me uncomfortable, I said, "The truth is I have nobody to go back to. I'll do whatever you say, Uncle Ramses."

"Just as I thought. My senses are never wrong."

He asked for my ID card and, after a moment, quietly stood up and bent over to pull out a large ledger from beneath his bed. It was olive green and had a huge white "A" on the cover. Ignoring me—maybe he thought I had dozed off—he opened it, and began turning some of its heavy pages, stopping every once in a while to run his index finger across some of the lines. Eventually he made an entry in pencil and looked at his watch. Then, sensing that I was observing him, he closed the heavy ledger with a thump.

"What does the "A" stand for?"

"What "A"?" he answered, slipping the book back beneath his bed.

Ramses opened the curtain to let in the early morning light. We would be heading to the church in a moment. But first, he prepped me on what to say and how to say it when we met Father Stephanos. He had me repeat everything to him word for word, with him playing the role of the priest. Essentially, it was the same story I had told the deputy public prosecutor. As we set off, he asked me for what must have been the third or fourth time whether I was married. I repeated what I had said a couple of hours earlier: my husband had died in Iraq.

Ramses' mouth curved back up into that strange smile and out of it came the last thing I had expected. "Well then, congratulations to the bride. Tayea's got a wedding to look forward to."

7

AFTER RAMSES TOOK HODA TO his cabin, I climbed back into bed. Staring up at the ceiling, I felt I was floating in the middle of the room. When it rains it pours. I'd had more weird experiences in less than twenty-four hours than in my whole three years with the public prosecutor's office in Cairo. True, this was my first rural posting, but that alone wouldn't account for this spate of disasters. Maybe the lodge was jinxed. I shuddered at the thought of ghosts and Ramses's stories. Hoda mentioned that she changed her name when she sought refuge at the mosque. But why did she choose "Nour" in particular? Did she and Ramses know each other? Were they playing some kind of trick on me? I found it hard to reconcile deceit with her angelic features. But then again, there was no denying she had lied about getting off the train at Tayea thinking it was Beni Soueif. This village has no train station. And why Beni Soueif if her actual destination was Assiut, as she claimed? I felt a sudden chill. I pulled my covers up, rolled onto my side and fell into a deep sleep, despite these disturbing thoughts that circled overhead like hungry crows.

My eyes shot open in alarm after only a couple of hours of sleep. I thought I heard a sound coming from the ground floor. I raced downstairs in my bare feet and pyjamas, calling for Ramses, but I received no answer. I pulled aside the curtains and saw him from afar, with Hoda a step or two behind him. They were heading in the direction of the church.

I flopped down on the leather couch in the living room, desperate for just a few more minutes of rest. Sleep answered my prayers grudgingly, granting me more than an hour of uneasy, but undisturbed rest. Despite the exhaustion I felt after all that happened on my first day here, I awoke at my habitual time.

Just as I was about to get into the car the district judiciary branch provided me, I caught sight of Ramses coming from the direction of the village. He was alone. He gestured for me to wait and, despite his age, broke into a run. As surprised as I was that he had returned sooner than expected, I ignored him. I climbed into the back seat and told the driver to get going. Ramses caught up with us before we passed the front gate.

"Way to go, sir!" he said, "The ruling you made last night. You've done us proud."

He was panting so hard, he could barely utter two words in a row, but his smile remained fixed and it seemed to have grown quite greasy all of a sudden.

I ordered the driver to stop.

"How did you hear about it? Who told you?"

"Nothing stays hidden for long in our village, sir. The clerk from your office told me. His name's Girgis. He's a cousin of mine. I just ran into him at the church a little while ago. Besides, the whole village has been talking about nothing else since sunup. You know, how Judge Radwan returned home at dawn with his tail between his legs."

I stared at him, at a loss for words. I was surrounded on all sides. I reached up and loosened my tie. I was about to change the subject and ask how it went with Hoda at the church, but then I noticed a strange-looking man next to the lodge. Both tall and thickset, he wore a dark woolen overcoat over his galabiya and had a large rifle slung over his shoulder. But the most remarkable feature was a red tarboosh that he had pressed so far down his forehead that it concealed half his face. He seemed to have stepped right out of Tawfiq al-Hakim's *Diary of a Country Prosecutor*. Noticing the direction of my gaze, Ramses volunteered proudly, "That's Nabawi Dib, the rest house guard, Sir."

"And where was this Nabawi Dib yesterday night when Madam Hoda paid us the honor?"

"In town, sir. He spends the night there and comes to work in the morning. Now Nabawi, there's a man with a tale to tell."

I showed no enthusiasm for hearing Nabawi's tale, but I signaled the man over and told him not to leave until I returned. Nabawi looked worried and he answered, almost in a squeak.

"You'll be back before sundown, right, sir?"

I gave a noncommittal nod and told the driver to get going. On the way to the courthouse, the driver told me the story of Nabawi Dib, without me asking. Evidently, he was in the employ of the Ministry of Justice as a guard and had been posted at the judges' lodge for many years. He refused to be transferred to another directorate because of an old feud that was pursuing him from Assiut.

"That's why he never spends the night at the lodge," the driver explained. "Around sunset, Ramses escorts him into town and keeps an eye out for anyone who might be lurking in the dark, ready to attack. Then, at the first light of dawn, Nabawi reports back to the lodge and doesn't take a step off the grounds until sunset. You know that other hut on the grounds? That's for the guard. But Nabawi never uses it because he's afraid to be alone."

The driver's voice couldn't compete with the cries of itinerant vendors and the roar of motorcycles, so he fell silent as we entered the village. About 500 meters before we reached the courthouse, we saw a large and angry crowd. It was impossible to make out what they were shouting, especially since the sheep and goats some of the farmers had brought with them compounded the din. The noise grew louder as we approached. Our progress slowed until eventually we were forced to stop at a roadblock. A senior police officer came toward us, walkie-talking in hand. A large gun hung from a holster on his right side and, judging from his insignia, he was a commander in the force. I rolled down my window and introduced myself.

"Well, you made it at last, sir, safe and sound," he said with a smile. "This roadblock's here for you, sir. If you'll just let me take charge of you—"

"What happened?"

"Nothing to worry about. It's just that ruling you made yesterday. Your decision to maintain the status quo upset Judge Radwan and his family and their supporters, as you can see. Now, if you would get out of the car, sir, and walk next to me calmly, we'll sneak you into the courthouse through the backdoor."

On the way, he explained to me the impact of the decision I'd taken in light of the local demographics. In contrast to the vast majority of Egyptian villages, Copts made up more than eighty percent of the population of Tayea. I listened to him without interrupting, while in the background I picked up chants about the lack of justice in the courts and the tyranny of the public prosecution. Every now and then the officer would pause to speak into his walkie-talkie to ensure his men were alert and the road ahead was safe, then resume. He refuted certain points in my ruling and explained how it jeopardized security. It was important to treat Muslims and Copts exactly the same, even if the Muslims were a minority. The Bishoi family obtained a usufruct for a plot of land last year, so this year it was the Radwan family's turn. The fact that the Muslims had more land than the Copts was beside the point. He concluded with an unsolicited piece of advice:

"You have to keep your sense of national security one step ahead of the law. As you know, sir, our work is ninety percent know-how and ten percent law."

I was treated to more of the same in my boss's office, albeit with a more judicious choice of words and the ratio of law rising to fifty percent. As though reading my thoughts on the lines of my furrowed brow, Mahmoud Bey concluded, "But enough of politics. Let's stick to legal matters. The Office of the Public Prosecutor has a hierarchical chain of command. What this means is that your superior takes the decisions and that you, Nader Bey, are a mere investigator."

I left his office, head bowed. I paused for a moment, then turned in the direction of my office. As I headed down the corridor, which was dim even though it was noon, I was preceded by a courthouse usher whose duty it was to order people to clear the way for me. Another usher followed, bellowing in regular intervals, "Move aside! Move aside! Make way for His

Honor." The way he stretched out his vowels made him sound like a foghorn. The first time he did that, I leaped to the wall on my right like the others.

"That wasn't meant for you, sir," the usher said.

I hope he took my foolish smile to mean I was just kidding.

I was assailed by piercing gazes from lawyers and litigants as I neared my office. I tried my best to ignore them, but I still felt myself shrink. The dignitary's procession I'd been granted all the way from my boss's office had fooled no one. No sooner did I settle into my chair than the clerk told me that the Radwan file had been given to a colleague. My exasperated sigh proclaimed to all within hearing range that I had already come to detest this village that had me running around breathless in the wilderness since the moment I set foot in it. If I hadn't been afflicted with the curse of Nour that Ramses had told me about, my faith was certainly being tested by adversity.

Over the next month, a tall stack of old case files remained piled on my desk. I had inherited them from the colleague whom I had replaced, but I hadn't had a moment to look at them because of the many fresh claims and complaints I had to deal with daily. One day, the label "Crimes against Persons," ornately inscribed on some of the folders, caught my attention. I picked out one, a murder case. I quickly drafted a summary of the incident report and interrogations conducted. Noticing that one of the suspects and some witnesses had not been questioned yet, I snapped the folder shut, tucked it under my arm and headed to my superior to ask how to proceed. I launched into a spirited brief, but in less than a minute, he held up his hand and said in an icy voice: "Handle it however you want. Don't come to me with something like this. It's routine: Mohammed kills Ahmed."

I reinserted the documents in the file, while he, without looking in my direction, added, "Just come to me with new cases. Don't take a single action on them before that, not even to make a note in the margins."

I nodded my assent, but I doubt he noticed. He must have sensed I would not object.

Back in my office, I plunked myself down on my chair, thumped the file on my desk, and ordered another cup of coffee. Girgis gave me a look that asked, "What's going on?" I smiled, then snatched up a piece of paper, scribbled the names of the witnesses on it, and handed it to him.

"Subpoena them all for tomorrow. I want to question them all at the same time so no one can change their story." As he reached the door, I added, "And let me know if any of them won't come willingly or are going to be late so I can charge them with contempt and issue a warrant for their arrest."

I was confident that Girgis would convey my instructions to the district police chief and that all the witnesses would be trembling before me the following day. Alone in my office, I stared at the wall, consumed by troubling thoughts about the concepts of justice and rule of law. I could hear my father's words to me the day I was hired by the Public Prosecutor's Office. He had retired from the judiciary just a few months previously. "Listen only to the voice of your conscience. When politics interfere with the judiciary, it corrupts. When the law interferes with politicians, it reforms."

I leaned my head back and closed my eyes until, suddenly, a loud rap on the door snapped me out of my reverie. A police sergeant stepped into the room, barked his name, gave a military salute, handed me a piece of paper, and stepped back to wait at attention. I unfolded the paper and stared at a scrawl that looked like several wavy lines of barbed wire. Apart from a word here or there, I could make out nothing. Noticing my confusion, the young man volunteered,

"It's a notification from the Giza Police Station, sir. They want a warrant for the arrest of a certain Mohammed Alwan Shaltout and a search warrant for his house. He's being charged with embezzling government property. They want our department to investigate."

As soon as he finished, Girgis entered and handed me the case file which had just arrived, along with instructions to follow up on the investigation. It was as though I was in a play in which the two of them performed their parts on cue. I quickly glanced through the papers and nearly burst out laughing. Turning to the office phone, I punched my boss's extension, and gave him a summary. His silence lasted for so long, I thought he might have hung up. Then he said,

"Run that by me again, please, and be succinct. This guy, Mohammed Alwan, he embezzled what?"

"A peacock, sir. Mohammed Alwan works at the zoo in Giza. He's accused of stealing a peacock and hiding it in his house here in Tayea."

8

THE ROAD TO THE VILLAGE'S main church was shorter than I'd expected. We walked halfway around the lodge and passed through a gate onto the road. Soon, we veered to the left, then to the left again, after which we took a sharp turn to the right. Suddenly, it stood before me, tall and majestic—the Church of El Nour, the Holy Light. I felt at peace all at once. There was a massive iron door without a guard, but Ramses led me around to a side door which he opened with a key of his own.

He left me waiting in a large room with no windows apart from a single narrow slit high up in the wall that let in some light. Growing impatient, I decided to look around. As soon as I started down the corridor, I saw a priest and, just behind him, Ramses. The priest was a large and impressive man. He smiled down at me gently and introduced himself. I kissed his extended hand and said, "May the Lord bless me with your sanctuary, Father."

After leading me back into the room and inviting me to have a seat, I started to tell him my story as I had rehearsed it, but Ramses signaled to me to remain silent.

"Are you married, my daughter?" the priest asked in a quiet voice.

"No, Father, I'm a widow."

51

"And what's your full name? May I see your ID?"

"My name's Hoda Yusef Habib, I'm 35, and my ID card's with Ramses."

"Now, tell me your story, daughter."

Although I was sure Ramses had already told him, I related how my stepfather had assaulted me and what happened to me at the guesthouse. After confirming that my late husband had died in Iraq, Father Stephanos accepted me into the service of the church. He lay his palm gently on my head and said, "Those whose hearts are with us in Tayea outnumber those who are against us. 'Thou shall not fear the terror of the night or the arrow that flies by day.' You'll find safety and peace here, daughter."

My duties were to clean the rooms in the annex that housed the children's classrooms. My sleeping quarters were in a small room located beneath the main stairway with two elderly women. This was because the other three churches were closed at present. "For repairs," Father Stephanos added in a voice thick with sarcasm. He raised his eyes heavenward and mouthed a prayer for deliverance.

Ramses bent toward the priest's ear to whisper something loud enough for me to hear. Father Stephanos turned to me and said, "Sure, why not? Let's see how she does teaching the children, as long as she has a certificate."

And so, thanks to a few words from Ramses, I was instantly promoted from cleaner to teacher. I thanked Father Stephanos and kissed his hand. But just before we left, Ramses whispered something else in his ear. This time it was too soft for me to hear, but whatever he said was also met with the Father's approval. He nodded and patted Ramses on the shoulder, saying "May the good Lord make it come to pass."

*

Less than a month after I had been given sanctuary at the church, Father Stephanos gave his blessing to my engagement to the church's electrician, Rizq. He must have been around ten years older than me, but he was still unmarried. This time, it was Ramses's will, instead of my mother's, that had spoken for mine. I didn't object because I owed him, though my heart was still pregnant with the dream of a nascent freedom, one that apparently would remain unborn.

On the day I married Rizq, memories of a similar occasion some years earlier raced through my mind. I stood facing Khidr, my mother, and her husband in a poorly lit room. Next to them sat a sheikh who didn't look at me once and who wasn't interested in hearing whether I consented or not. Earlier, they had forced me to authorize the man who had raped me to give me away in marriage to the man next in line. After the sheikh entered my name and age in the ledger, they led me to the guillotine. Day after day, Khidr would execute me over and over again in his bed. There was no difference between that marriage and being led to the gallows. The rites and rituals were similar: a recitation of my sins, prayers for the Lord's guidance and forgiveness, and a train of cold eyes escorting me to my fate. The solitude was the same. I felt like screaming, "I'm innocent," but I had learned to remain silent.

In my church wedding I was also alone, but it didn't feel the same. I wished my family could have been there to see Rizq present me my bridal gift: a gold necklace with a gold cross as a pendant. I had never received a bridal gift before. Nor had I ever worn a white wedding dress, as I did that evening. If only my father were alive. He would have visited the following morning bearing cages of fowl and he would have come again on the third day, bringing his older brother to slaughter a calf. I could picture my late uncle followed by his donkey pulling a cart filled with sacks of wheat, rice, and vegetables for my new home. Of course, my mother would have visited too during the first two days. She would've brought Rizq and me sweets, baked goods, and asked Rizq's mother to present me with one of her abayas as a token of affection for her new daughter-in-law. If only Rizq could know that I had a family that loved and supported me, that I was more than just a woman of child-bearing age that Ramses had donated to the church.

"This is your cross for you to bear for the rest of your life," said Father Stephanos, interrupting my thoughts. He was addressing Rizq, and I knew he meant that divorce was forbidden. "What God has joined together let no man put asunder." He looked at me, and I nodded automatically. Nothing could be worse than my experience with Khidr. I caught sight of Ramses, who was still grinning, as he had been from the moment we entered the church that day. For the fourth or fifth time, I wanted to ask him what he had to gain from my marriage to Rizq, but I knew I would get little more than that smile.

That evening my husband hosted our wedding party in his home. He invited all his neighbors, both Copts and Muslims. You can't tell the difference in times of joy and celebration. I sat among a crowd of women, girls, and children in the courtyard. They were all strangers to me. They showered me with affection, but I felt no warmth. Some men were beating drums while others clapped rhythmically, and the women ululated intermittently. Ululations are supposed to be joyful cries, but to me they sounded like wails. I forced myself to keep a faint smile on my face the whole evening, but if anyone had looked at me closely or had taken a picture of me, my eyes would have given me away.

I moved to Rizq's house at the edge of town from the small bedroom I had shared with the elderly ladies at the church. It was at the beginning of the road to the main market, so everyone passed it on their way there.

It was also quite a distance from the four churches that surrounded the little mosque in a gentle embrace, as though to preserve it. Sheikh Ragab didn't see it that way. On Fridays, it was impossible to shut out the sheikh's fulminations against us, despite the distance. He always turned up the mosque's loudspeaker full blast. They couldn't just leave us in peace, that was life and one just had to accept it. I had to admit that some folks in the church said just as nasty things about them as they did about us, but we were never as flagrant about it as they were. In his Friday sermons, he railed about how the mosque was surrounded and prevented from expanding. State Security had cautioned him several times against igniting strife, but the warnings were "toothless," as Father Stephanos put it. They pass by his place to give him a word of advice or make a request. They might even issue a warning once in a while, but it's too diffident. It's like shooting into the air without making a sound because the words have never been backed up by action of any sort. With time, it became clear to Sheikh Ragab that those were just warning shots, performed for duty's sake, but never meant to harm. If anything, they probably encouraged him to keep going.

One morning we awoke to find that someone had painted a large black cross on our front door. Maybe it was to distinguish it from the homes of our Muslim neighbors down the road. Rizq cleaned it off, but they came back before dawn the next day and painted it on again. They did the same day after day until it seemed pointless to remove it.

When I told Ramses about the problem, he advised me to file a complaint at the Public Prosecutor's Office and to name my next-door neighbor. He said that Hajj Mohammed Alwan had wanted to buy our house when its owner, a Muslim man, passed away, but Rizq beat Alwan to it. I found this hard to believe. Mohammed was a kind, good-natured man who always greeted me warmly. He was also old and had a beautiful, well-kept home. Ramses kept up a steady buzz in my ear about how Alwan and his wife had a blind hatred for Copts. One day, when he didn't get the reaction he wanted from me, he said that Alwan and his wife were working black magic against me. "He brings strange bird feathers from the zoo in Giza where he works. His wife dips them in oil mixed with black nigella seeds and a chicken carcass, and he scatters them in front of your house. Everyone knows that's to ruin your home, make you poor and miserable, cause fights between you and your husband, and bind him so you can't bear children."

He paused for a moment to study my face with his bulging eyes, then added in a low voice, "By the way, his wife's called Hoda too. Now, why would people call you the Coptic woman and her by her name?"

I began to scan the area in front of our threshold every day, first thing in the morning. Some days later I found a long, gray, strangely shaped feather. I picked it up and ran my finger down the edge. It was smooth to the touch. My heart sank. It occurred to me to wipe the cross off my door and paint one on Alwan's door to let him know I was on to him. But even if I had, it would have been too late.

Before long, people began to refer to our home not as Rizq's place but as the Coptic woman's house, which was strange because all the other houses in Tayea were named after their men. Our house had become a landmark. If anyone from out of town got lost on their way to the public market, which was held every Tuesday and Thursday, locals would point them toward our road and tell them, "Just ask for the Coptic woman's house. It's right after that." I could erase the cross from our door, but I couldn't erase "Coptic woman's house" from the tongues of the Muslims in our village.

I kept the feathers I found. I dipped them in water with some bluing liquid, made the sign of the cross over them to cancel the spell, then put them in front of Alwan's doorstep. He never touched them. Rizq's affection for our neighbors never diminished. The cross on our door remained. People continued to call the Muslim Hoda, Hoda, without epithets. I kept my thoughts to myself. Silence seemed a more practical solution than crying. At least I had made that choice with my own free will for a change.

Then one day, Mohammed Alwan took off from his roof like a bird on fire, and the whole of Tayea went up in flames.

9

I SAT AT MY DESK, pen in hand, doodling. I drew a triangle. At its base were the custodians of justice: judges and public prosecutors, of which I was one. One leg consisted of lawyers for the litigants—the "standing judiciary," as they liked to call themselves. The other leg was short and lame. It consisted of all the people pursuing their rights in the courts as plaintiffs and even defendants. The image of Lady Justice sprang to mind. I wondered about the sculptor who had rendered justice as a blindfolded woman carrying a scale: how was she to keep her scales balanced? We're supposed to believe the blindfold means she can't discriminate between adversaries in court, but I think that sculptor must have experienced such a nightmarish trek through the labyrinth of courts in some bygone era that he concluded justice was blind to both his rights and his plight.

I went to the window and looked out over the vast expanse of nothingness, the fields that stretched on forever. In the distance, tiny red squares, like matchboxes, dotted the horizon. They were too small to see clearly, but I knew they were the villagers' houses. Some palm trees swayed in the autumn breeze. Their calm and regular rhythm jarred with the blare of the loudspeaker from the nearby mosque. Sheikh Ragab was giving a sermon following the afternoon prayers, forcing everyone in the village to listen to his grating voice.

The solar disk grew a deeper yellow before reddish tinges spread out and turned it orange. As the sun dipped below the horizon, all God's creatures fell silent apart from the sheikh, who continued with a lowered voice, even at such a sacred moment that commands only reverent meditation. I have always marveled at the slowly shifting hues of that divine landscape that unfolds itself before us day after day.

My thoughts were interrupted by a loud rap on the door, followed by the click of government boots, and a booming voice. "Sir!" said Sergeant Ismail with a stiff salute. "We've arrested the suspect Mohammed Alwan, sir."

I cleared my head of the worries that had pursued me since my arrival in Tayea, or Tayha as they call it here—as Ramses said, it made no difference; the "obedient" one is eternally "lost"—and focused with growing amazement on the man standing just outside the door. Mohammed Alwan was nearing sixty. The protruding bones of his clavicle and rib cage proclaimed his poverty. Yet, he'd married for a second time two years ago, and to a woman thirty years younger than him and attractive as well. She stood next to him, dazed and confused. I invited her inside along with him, but she remained two steps behind him with her head bowed. Her bashfulness struck me as contrived. What might explain that improbable marriage? He had no money or standing. He was just a low-ranking employee at the Giza Zoo, tasked with guarding the peacocks. He set off to work at 5:00 a.m. and returned exhausted twelve hours later. What was so attractive about that? Perhaps it had to do with the fact that he'd inherited a house in the village from his father. He also owned a couple of plots of land, totaling about a tenth of an acre, which he rented out. But that would give him barely enough to scrape by—or wouldn't it?

I mistakenly asked him that very question, albeit as delicately as I could phrase it. Alwan flushed. "God provides," he said, barely audible.

His wife was not encumbered by such timidity. She shed the demureness, arched an eyebrow, and said in a voice filled with contempt,

"So, is it illegal now to make an honest living?"

I asked Alwan to take a seat and told his wife to wait outside. She swung around and exited with a sashay, no less. I shook my head and returned to the case file, and once again I was overcome by the astonishment that struck me when I first opened it. Most of the incident had taken place in the zoo after closing time, but the spark came from Tayea. Apparently, the new wife wanted proof that her husband would continue to love her, having turned down very many other suitors before him. She had let her heart prevail over her mind, which had told her that a woman of her youth, beauty, and shapely body deserved a better life than he promised, at least materially, when she had said, "If you truly love me, fetch me a peacock from the zoo, tonight."

Or at least that was how I imagined the conversation went. She wanted a token of undying love and he was going to give her one, come hell or high water. The rest I had to fill in myself. That's as far as my imagination could take me; I'm a lawyer, not a novelist, as much as I like to read fiction. I flicked a cigarette out of my pack, lit it, and narrowed my eyes at Alwan. It was time to get into character as an investigator for the prosecution and pry the rest of the story from him.

"The evidence is stacked against you," I said in a cold, menacing tone. "The smart thing to do is confess. The law will be easier on you."

He nodded several times, as though to confirm what the slumped shoulders and doleful eyes had already said: the rabbit gives up the fight when caught in the lion's jaws. As he related his tale, the dejection in his voice struck me as a kind of reproach, as though to say, "You could have saved yourself the trouble. I would have spoken up on my own accord."

Alwan recounted how, after racking his brain for hours, he came up with a plan. He bought an overcoat that was so large for him it flapped out like a tent on his scrawny frame. Shortly before the end of his shift, he used the coat to trap the peacock. Then he administered a tranquilizer dart strong enough to put the bird into a sound sleep for several hours. He then wrapped it loosely in a length of fabric, secured it around his waist, and left at the end of his shift. At the main gate, he bid goodnight to a guard who failed to notice how his belly had suddenly swelled like a woman in her ninth month of pregnancy.

As Mohammed spoke, I tried to picture that poor peacock in a setting it would never have imagined in the bleakest hours of its confinement in the zoo. Its groggy eyes would have opened to a small courtyard in a humble rural home on the outskirts of Tayea, and to an attractive country woman in a galabiya with slits up the sides. It would have been spellbound for a moment by the ankle bracelet, but that glittery ornament wouldn't have been able to compete with the sparkling eyes of the woman. Her pride and heart had just been rewarded, prompting her to plant a tender kiss on Mohammed Alwan's cheek as he removed his overcoat, chest puffed from his victorious hunting trip, perhaps the first of its kind in the history of Egypt.

It wasn't hard to deduce the rest of the story. Two days later, the zoo management discovered a female peacock was missing—probably because the male, deprived of his mate, was making such a racket. All concerned agencies moved into action, as state-run newspapers reported, and police investigations were conducted with the utmost diligence. The Chief Investigator Colonel got involved, under the supervision of the Director of Investigations Brigadier General, in collaboration with the Major General and Police Commissioner of Giza, and under the watchful eye of His Excellency the Minister of Interior. Thanks to these concerted efforts, the poor peacock guard was startled out of his sleep by State Security Intelligence agents banging on his door at dawn. After a quick search, the agents left bearing both the prey and the prize.

They presented me with a large, mustard-colored, government-issue evidence envelope. It bulged, but weighed almost nothing, and its flap was secured with a red wax seal. In my capacity as deputy public prosecutor, I opened it, eying my prey whose eyes darted back and forth to evade my gaze, and extracted several long feathers belonging to the missing peacock.

"The items I'm exhibiting to you here were confiscated from your home in your presence. What do you have to say?" I said sternly, still in character.

"I'll say whatever you tell me to say, sir."

I remained silent.

"They're a bunch of feathers, sir. I told you I'm the one who stole the peacock. I confessed to everything. So I'm not going to turn around and say those aren't its feathers."

"Good. So, where's the peacock?"

His eyes welled as he patted his belly. Choking on his tears, he explained that his infatuation with his second wife is what drove him to commit this crime. She, in turn, rewarded him by slaughtering the purloined bird in tribute to his courage. The next thing he knew, its stewed joints were set before him in a bowl, swimming in a thick green broth.

I gasped, "You ate it in molokhia?"

He nodded, head bowed in remorse.

Despite the streaming tears that glistened on his cheeks and moistened the front of his galabiya, I smiled and then, unable to contain myself, I burst out laughing.

The problem was that under the law, Mohammed Alwan faced up to fifteen years in prison with hard labor, plus a hefty fine and the loss of his job. Technically, the poor wretch before me was guilty of embezzlement. He was a government employee who, in accordance with his duties, had been entrusted with a public asset, and he abused his authority. The law does not discriminate between an embezzler of millions of pounds and an embezzler of a peacock. Justice is blind.

The moment I stepped out of my office, the two police conscripts, assigned to clear my way down judiciary corridors, jumped to their feet. I raised my hand like a traffic cop, signaling them to stay put, then pinned them to their wooden chairs with a deterrent glare. I couldn't stomach the loud charade of a dignitary's procession to my boss's office. I spread open the record of Alwan's interrogation on the district prosecutor's desk and took a seat. He grunted and gave the document a cursory scan until he came to the part about the molokhia with peacock. He laughed as loudly as I did, then shut the file.

"Excellent," he said as he handed it back to me. "Now just finish up the paperwork and go get yourself a couple of hours of sleep. You'll be taking the night shift."

"But what should I do about Mohammed Alwan?"

"Jail, of course. Embezzlement of public assets. He was vested with a public trust and he breached it. That's a felony and he's guilty. You got a problem with that?"

"But he's an old man and he's got heart problems. And he'll lose his job—"

"If he's old and sick and needs work, what's he doing committing a crime at work? In fact, what's he doing marrying a girl half his age?"

Mahmoud Bey must have taken my extended silence for assent, because he turned back to his work. I abruptly set the file back on his desk and said, "I know you're going to remind me about the chain of command, but I'm not going to lock that man up. If that's what you want, here's the file. I'm not going to have that man's fate on my conscience."

I stood to leave, but my dumbstruck boss quickly regained his composure and asked me to sit down again. He picked up his phone to have his secretary get us some coffee and offered me a cigarette. Then he lowered his voice, though there was no one in the room to hear us except for the devil perhaps, and said, "Don't be so stubborn. Do you have another solution?"

"Sure. We refer his file to the administrative prosecution and recommend a disciplinary penalty, such as dismissal, then we close the case as a criminal investigation."

"Agreed," my boss said as though glad to be relieved of the burden. "But on the condition we also propose that the government deduct half of his monthly pension until he's paid off the debt for the peacock."

I agreed, despite my concerns for the man's age, his illness and his dismissal, all of which were, to me, ample reasons for simply closing the investigation. In the end, the defendant had to pay for the most expensive dish of molokhia in his life and maybe in the history of Egyptian cuisine. But at least he was spared prison and complete destitution.

I released Mohammed Alwan, inserting a hundred pound note in the pocket of his galabiya as tears of gratitude streamed down his cheeks. Afterwards, I continued to keep tabs on him through Ramses, who assured me Alwan was well and had enough money to spend, and lavishly. Ramses also told me that the people of Tayea disapproved the ruling to release Alwan. I didn't believe him. I couldn't conceive of a reason for their disapproval, and Ramses never bothered to explain.

Not long afterward, Ramses told me that Alwan's situation had taken a turn for the worse. His wife had left him and obtained a divorce. Nobody knew why. Sometime after that, Ramses told me, with more than a hint of malicious glee, the charming divorcée remarried. Her new husband was the brother of the current mayor, Abduh Tayea.

I lost interest in the subject until one day, while we were on the veranda, I saw a large and beautiful bird in the yard which reminded me of the peacock.

"How's Mohammed Alwan doing?" I asked.

Ramses' face grew visibly tense.

"It seems like he was struck by the curse of Nour."

"Nour? Nour who?"

"Have you forgotten, sir? Nour, the daughter of Mohammed Tayea, the village's first mayor and the grandfather of Abduh Tayea, our current mayor. The beautiful Nour appeared to Alwan in a dream like a djinn then flew off in a blaze of flame. He got up at dawn, went up to his roof, and set himself on fire to follow her. May his soul rest in peace."

"When did this happen, Ramses?"

"A couple of days ago. Your colleague, Osman Bey, is investigating the incident. May God have mercy on your soul, Alwan. May He forgive you for stealing that bird and eating stolen food."

Ramses fell silent and turned his focus to turning the corncobs, while I stared off into space. When I turned to him again, I caught a gleam in his eyes that sent a chill up my spine. His whole face seemed to fade apart from those two large eyes. Heaven help us, I thought.

"How did you know she visited him in a dream?" I asked.

He shot me a reproachful smile.

"They all go the same way," he said with the assurance of someone familiar with arcane secrets of the universe. "They go up to their roofs and set fire to themselves. Then the wind blows them down to the ground, like a bird in flames, sir. Alwan wasn't the first, and he won't be the last as long as the curse of Nour hangs over us. She was the first one to do that, but she vanished. Since then, if she appears to anyone in a dream, they follow her example. She calls them to her."

Unconsciously, my hand felt for my empty gun. Looking at those frightening eyes that jarred with that permanent smile, I said, "First thing tomorrow morning, I want you to pass by the station and submit an ammunition requisition. I want at least fifty bullets."

I ignored the questioning look he gave me.

10

KHIDR MANGLED MY SOUL. HIS daily assaults on my body and my emotions, his determination to imprison and break them both, made me hate both and lose all hope of ever finding warmth and affection. He destroyed my youth with his relentless degradation and shredded my dreams to the point I could no longer piece them together. I was the moon, flooding the sky with tears, and the stars were the lusterless pearls that fell from my eyes every night. In the end, I killed him. He found peace and left me to my misery.

The people in the village called my house the Coptic woman's house. The name and the implications bothered me, but Rizq embraced me with his kindness and gave me strength. I still feared him as a man. When he approached, I cringed and went rigid, or shook uncontrollably and broke into tears. He kept his distance to reassure me, but still I backed away as images of my step-father and Khidr flashed to mind. Yet every day he showed me affection. When he added a prayer for me in each of his seven daily prayers, it was like a life-giving breath from his soul.

The moment he first told me he had fallen in love with me, a thread of warmth bound him to my heart. His large eyes held mine and consoled me. My body trembled, but his hands curved around my waist relaxed me. He drew closer without invading me. He touched me gently, cautiously. He desired me. I could read that in his eyes. He let his love embrace me while he awaited my consent. He never tried to rush me. One night I gave him a flirtatious smile, and his whole face beamed.

"How about we play a game of strip poker?" he asked, like a mischievous child.

I laughed so hard my eyes watered. I couldn't remember when I had last laughed from my heart. I was still shy and apprehensive. I wanted to hold him, but I was feeling my way. I didn't want to lose him. I was afraid that if I drew any closer, I might come to hate him. So I stayed in that no-man's land between happiness and playing safe, unable to drink from the well of the former, and parched in the desert of fear. My only consolation was that the desert sun was setting.

Rizq, sitting on the bed with his legs folded beneath him, shuffled the deck excitedly and began to arrange the cards. He had taken my laughter for assent. I was scared to lose. Yet when my mind strayed to the penalty, I couldn't concentrate and lost one round after the next. The victory brought a sparkle to his eyes, and behind that there was a strange gleam that excited me and made my head feel light. He didn't insist on the winner's rights. They can wait, his gentle smile told me. I lay down on my back and closed my eyes. My body trembled for a moment, then relaxed as he took me into his embrace and held me to his chest. I felt myself flow between his ribs, bask in the warmth of his feelings, and sway to the rhythm of his heart. I wept as he held me in his arms and sang softly. The gentle hum rocked us into a deep sleep until morning.

Rizq eventually managed to erase the scars left by Khidr. For the first time in my life, I felt what it was like to feel pleasure as a woman. I sighed contentedly and turned to him with a smile. I hadn't had my fill of him yet. He lay on his back, his chest heaving but beginning to relax. He looked at me out of the corner of his eyes and opened his arms, inviting me back into his embrace. I accepted the invitation, wrapped my arms around him, and hugged him. He held me in return and stroked my hair. "I've been rewarded for my patience," he said softly. "If I hadn't put off marrying, I would never have met you."

I rested my head on his chest, wishing I could melt into it and never have to leave. He caressed my back with his large hand. I playfully pressed my body closer while the sole of my foot curved around his leg and stroked it, delicately exploring that unfamiliar surface. Rizq began to breathe more rapidly. He returned my caresses and joined his body to mine for another passionate adventure.

I became a butterfly driven to the flame to burn its sin, even though I chose to flutter through fields of flowers. I shook my head to clear it of such thoughts. This was not a sin. I was just troubled by what I was hiding from Rizq. I could never bring myself to tell him how I had accidentally killed my first husband. Rizq showered me with so much kindness and affection. He satisfied me in every way, and when I thirsted for more, he quenched that thirst. I grew more radiant and more worried at the same time. He was forty-five, even if he didn't look it, and he was desperate to have children. I longed to be a mother too, though there were no signs of that happening. He pretended not to care, but his eyes gave him away. There was a faint shimmer of sadness that only I could detect. One night,

71

I held his head in my hands and brought my face closer to his. Some tears escaped and I wiped them away. Then I hugged him and listened to us breathing in harmony.

Speaking softly, I said, "It will work, I swear by the Holy Virgin, it will be a boy. But please be patient and don't leave me."

"Leave you? I can barely believe I found you. You're my soul's soul. How could I ever leave you?"

He kissed the palms of my hand, my neck, my cheeks, and my lips. I clutched him to me and we melted into a long embrace. Afterwards, we lay on our backs, panting and smiling, as though we had just finished a friendly battle that had sapped and fired our passions all at once.

Rizq yawned like a gentle-hearted child, pulled the covers up and before long his breathing settled into the rhythm of sleep. My worries loomed up again to torment me. I feared the Lord was keeping me from bearing children as a way to punish me for hiding the truth about my former marriage. But I had never meant to kill Khidr.

Soon after I moved in with Rizq, our neighbors began to think I had some kind of magical power, simply because coincidence had arranged for me to be present when fate worked its miracles. Why people attributed them to me instead of to a higher power is beyond me.

Rizq's sister, Sara, had given birth prematurely. The infant seemed nearly lifeless and the doctor at the clinic said he probably wouldn't live. She pleaded with me to pray for her son and give him my benediction. I hesitated. People had begun to expect more and more from me each day and I hardly needed another painful reminder that I, myself, was unable to have children. Nevertheless, I placed my hand on the infant's head and prayed. Two hours later, Sara's son kicked his tiny feet. If he hadn't, they would have buried him. All at once, the wailing turned to ululations, and tears of joy swept aside tears of despair over the long-awaited newborn.

The rumor spread like wildfire that I had invoked the spirit of the Lord Jesus and brought the dead infant back to life. Thanks to my intercession, our Savior appeared, embraced the child, and fended off the Angel of Death. I had done nothing more than utter a few prayers, but my reputation as a miracle worker grew until women not just from Tayea, but from nearby towns and villages too, came to me so they could bear sons. Stranger yet, many visitors to the "Coptic woman's house" were Muslim women, whom I welcomed, of course.

The sound of rustling leaves grew louder and made me shiver. The howling wind urged me to get up, go back to the bedroom and climb under the blankets. I took a sip from my tea, hoping it would give me some warmth. I looked out the window. It was so dark outside, I could barely make out the palm of my hand. The cold bit into my bones even though I had bundled myself up in heavy clothes and shawls, and covered my head, ears, and feet. I gave a long yawn, as though it might summon sleep more quickly so I could join Rizq, who had gone to bed early. I stood up, then froze when I caught sight of the ghostlike figure of a masked man racing between the houses. A fat, slow moving man was carrying a bucket and struggling to keep up. I didn't budge. They stopped some distance away. I squinted, trying to make them out more clearly. The masked man's eyes glowed like those of a huge black cat.

I turned at a soft noise behind me. Rizq had woken up to drink a glass of water. He pulled his black woolen blanket more snugly around him, squatted down next to me, and began to trace crosses in the air and mutter prayers.

"Do you see what I see out there, Rizq?"

He gave me a long tender look, then he stood up sleepily, saying he saw nothing. He adjusted his blanket again and repeated something he had told me before.

"People here don't like to file complaints with the police or tell the government their grievances."

He went back to bed and pulled the covers up over his head. I had picked up an unusual sternness in his tone, one that told me not to press him with more questions. Maybe he felt there were things I shouldn't know, or feared that curiosity would kill the cat.

I turned back to the ghostly figures, but they had vanished. I spotted the water tank with the cross on it which Ramses had brought us a couple of days ago. He told me to sprinkle water from it in front of Christian houses to ward off the Muslims' magic. I was skeptical for no reason I could think of. I opened it. It was filled to the brim with what looked like water, but it had a faint strange odor, like kerosene.

A shiver ran up my spine. I shut the windows firmly and double-checked the lock on the door. As I climbed into bed, the image of Ramses in a mask continued to haunt me until eventually weariness and fear forced my eyes shut. I fell asleep holding Rizq's hand beneath the blanket. It did not keep the nightmares from invading my sleep. I saw Ramses order me to sprinkle the kerosene water. The homes I sprayed with water suddenly burnt to flames. In the midst of all of it stood men, painting crosses on doors and laughing loudly. The flames never touched them.

The following morning, I saw another cross painted on Mohammed Alwan's house, which had remained closed since his death. Shocked at the sight, I related my nightmares to Rizq and told him about the cross. He shrugged what I said off with the same strange indifference I had noticed the night before.

"That's not a surprise. The news must have gotten out," he said as he resumed packing his electrician's gear in his work bag.

"What news?"

"The church bought his house and land from his children."

11

"YOU CAN'T KEEP THE PEACE with people who set their neighbors' fields on fire," Ramses said defiantly to the district police chief and the state security officer. Some officials in civilian dress were there, too. I didn't recognize any of them, but when they left the burnt fields, the rest of the uniformed police scurried after them.

Tayea had been frantic and on edge for several weeks. Fields belonging to Copts were being set on fire every other day, especially those bordering the Muslim fields. Only rarely did the reverse occur. Police said Muslim crops stored in the fields were also damaged by the fires, but Ramses told us the police made that up, and we believed him. This all came soon after Mohammed Alwan—the "peacock thief," as everyone had called him—committed suicide in such a horrifying way. It reminded the villagers of the wave of deadly arson attacks committed before I arrived in the village. There had been no threats or feuds, no advanced warning of any sort, which led people to believe that it was evil djinns who set the homes on fire while the people slept. Ramses said that was probably true, because the police never found any suspects and, as a result, all the cases went cold.

Rizq, his sister, and I were on our way to mass when the church bell started to chime insistently. With a sense of foreboding, we picked up our pace. As we neared the church, we saw Father Stephanos, Ramses, and the deacons and other young servants of the church standing in front of it. They stared angrily in the direction of the new annex. Flames leaped out of the windows, defying attempts to douse them. The police had cordoned off the area around the church. All roads leading to it had been blocked off, preventing the hundreds of people gathered outside from storming it. They were shouting insults and burning wooden crosses. Rizq took hold of my hand and drew me closer to him.

According to Ramses, who was answering everyone's questions, some people in the crowd had thrown petrol bombs over the outer fence and into the new building. No one knew why this had occurred. Then I noticed he was gone, even though he had been speaking to Rizq and me only a moment before. We went up to the police and asked them to let us through the cordon. They refused. We asked the senior officer, whose set jaw and scowl conveyed the same meaning. Noticing us, Father Stephanos stepped forward and intervened on our behalf.

We barely made it inside. I felt hands on my clothes trying to grope me. My stomach lurched violently, but I stayed silent. I didn't want Rizq to get riled up. Once inside the safety of the church grounds, the crowd's chants grew louder. The officer told us to keep calm, yet we were the ones who were surrounded.

They put out the fire in the annex, but not the one in our hearts. Father Stephanos listened to the security officers and officials without saying a word. One of them reproached him for trying to build a church without a permit. The priest explained that the new building was not a church but an annex for various functions. There was a lot of back-and-forth, most of which I couldn't follow, but then the state security officer said something about the "preservation of national unity."

The man next to him nodded several times and repeated reverently, "National unity. Yes, we must preserve national unity." He was the parliamentary representative from this district.

Father Stephanos turned to him and snapped, "National unity or dereliction of duty?"

Then the lights went out. We heard several shots followed by screams from the other side of the fence. Some people in the crowd lit the lamps they had with them. Two or three of the men outside had been shot and lay bleeding on the ground. One of the victims, a police conscript, died instantly. The crowd went wild and surged forward, pushing against the cordon of police, who, in turn, forcefully drove them back.

The church servants huddled protectively around Father Stephanos and bundled him into the church. The rest of us followed. Rizq and I were among the last ones in. The crowd's chants and shouts were crystal clear: they threatened revenge for the men who had just been shot and for Alwan before them.

I caught sight of Ramses near the baptismal font. The ladder leading to the loft was right behind him. His clothes were dusty, his chest heaved, and he had that same faint smile on his face. He was speaking excitedly to some young men around him. It seemed as though he was reproaching them, but I couldn't make out for what. The moment I drew near, he shut up and shot the others a warning look.

Rizq asked the question that was on my mind, as though afraid to hear the answer.

"Who fired the gun from above, Ramses?"

"How would I know?" he said, but he didn't look Rizq in the eyes.

"Why are the people outside talking about avenging Alwan?" I asked.

Ramses answered coldly, "Because the prosecution exhumed his body and did another autopsy."

"But what's that got to do with us?"

"They say he was strangled first and then set on fire. The Muslims say we're responsible.

For a week afterward, Rizq and I were so anxious and upset by the powder keg around us that we would lie side by side on our large bed at night, staring at the ceiling, like a pair of wooden caskets. The worry and insomnia that preyed on us all night eventually delivered us to the light of day and the mill of fear. The cycle continued to gnaw at us until, one day, we learned that the prosecution and police had closed the investigation on Alwan and the three men who had been shot and died in front of the church. Not a single Copt had been arrested and charged, and without suspects, the investigation reached a dead end. Eventually people forgot the matter, or so I thought.

"It's not as if people don't have other things to think about," Rizq said, his mouth curving into that mischievous smile I knew well. He held his arms out to me and said, "The living are more deserving than the dead, as they say."

I laughed and blushed like a virgin on her wedding night. I slid into his arms and surrendered to my emotions. Our souls and bodies fused as we hungrily compensated for our seven days of drought and sorrow.

I left the house before noon, walked a little way, and turned left toward the market. I could hear Rizq's voice as clearly as though he were walking right beside me: "Don't go to Muslim markets and stores. We should keep our distance." He had said that frequently since the events at the church.

I didn't go near al-Ezba al-Bahariya or the small mosque. I did not want to relive the painful memories of my arrival in Tayea, but images of that night in the mosque's guesthouse came to me unbidden. Lost in these thoughts, I shook my head to clear it. Suddenly, I felt the sound of squealing tires come fast at me from behind. I jumped, and heard someone shout, "*Humara!* You blind ass!"

I turned to see a man leaning half way out the window of his truck, flailing his arm at me angrily. His eyes widened and his mouth gaped. Mine did too, but I quickly adjusted my headscarf to conceal half my face as I struggled to stay calm. I picked up my pace, looking to my right, away from the road. As hard as I tried not to, I couldn't help stealing a look back. He stood outside the open door of his pickup, scratching the back of his head. He was about to take off after me. He would have caught me too, if he hadn't been held back by the blaring horns from the line of cars that were held up behind him.

It was Hilal, Khidr's elder brother. There was no doubt about it. He hadn't wanted Khidr to marry me. He hadn't wanted any sons of a Copt—that was how he referred to me— to become Khidr's heirs. Hilal only had daughters. What was he doing here in Tayea? I hastened on my way, looking behind quickly to see if he was still there. The traffic had returned to normal and there was no sign of his pickup.

An eerie calm hung over the market. There were not many vendors out even though it was midday. A sense of dread surged inside me and sunk its claws into my stomach. I kept looking behind me and searching the faces of people near me for Hilal. I almost turned to go back home, but I was too afraid and my knees felt shaky. So, instead, I decided to continue through the market to the other end. From there I would go to the church. Suddenly from afar, I spotted Salib Labib, the sweet potato seller, racing toward me, pushing his cart. He was terrified and yelling, but I couldn't make out what he was shouting until he had come closer. He hurtled past me, almost brushing my right side. Behind him, a tall young man in a black galabiya and black turban was chasing after him like the angel of death. The guy stopped to my left, raised a short rifle and fired two shots, one right after the other. Salib screamed and stumbled forward onto his wooden cart. The cart rolled several feet forward, leaving Salib sprawled face down on the ground. He was completely still and blood gushed out of his back.

Before I knew it, the market had turned into a battlefield. People screamed and ran this way and that. Men attacked each other with canes and sticks. Kids pelted one another with stones. Curses and obscenities flew in all directions. I raced to Salib's mother's house, which was nearby. I heard wailing inside. She must have heard how her son had just been killed and that no one had tried to help him.

I knocked and tried to enter, but the door had been barricaded shut. I called out to Umm Salib to let her know it was me, then managed to push open the door just wide enough for me to squeeze through. Three women, garbed all in black, were wailing and slapping their cheeks in grief, while Umm Salib struggled to lift another large sack onto the first two that were blocking the door. Without thinking, I rushed forward to help. After we barricaded the door with seven sacks filled with flour, Umm Salib and I flopped down on the floor, resting our backs against the sacks, chests heaving. I was as exhausted as her even though she was quite a bit older than me. I reached up to touch the golden cross on my chest and muttered a prayer to the Virgin Mary. That was when I noticed the opening above us. We were in a small courtyard where household chores would be carried out. Umm Salib and I looked at each other in alarm. She jerked her head upward as though to say, "That's how they'll attack."

Right then, a voice boomed over a screechy microphone, making an echo that increased our terror.

"Umm Salib, convert and find peace in Islam. They'll kill you if you don't pronounce the declaration of faith!"

Umm Salib leapt to her feet, suddenly filled with the energy of a girl quarter of her age, and shouted loud enough to be heard over the man's blaring voice:

"Let them kill us, Khalifa. I'll die a Copt, true to the faith of our Father in Heaven and to Christ our savior."

No reply came, and instead, some men outside began to pound and push against the door. It shook violently and seemed about to be wrenched off its hinges, but it held firm, thanks to our barricade. Then the pounding stopped, and all we heard were the sounds of women wailing and children screaming and crying.

I leapt to my feet, as though summoned by an inner voice, rushed to a large metal wash pan filled with water, and dragged it to the center of the room, right to the middle of

12

THE NIGHT FELT HEAVY, WRAPPED in a suspicious silence, as though no longer able to bear the strain of keeping a secret. Thin tendrils of dawn began to infiltrate the darkness. Diffused at first, they quickly took advantage of the night's final hesitation to flood the horizon with daylight. I became conscious of the phone ringing with growing persistence, as though it had been ringing for a while. I heard Nabawi's voice, but I could barely understand a word he said. Then I felt Ramses's hand on my shoulder, shaking it to wake me up. I cracked open an eye.

"The station called, sir. There's been a murder."

I rubbed my eyes hard and looked at the clock. It was five-thirty in the morning. I yawned. Ramses continued with an urgency meant to coax me to my feet.

"One of those Muslims killed Salib Labib in the market. Four people were wounded and are in critical condition."

The howling wind drew my attention to the view outside my window. The crests of the trees bowed to their creator. A lone farmer heading toward the village pulled his wooden coat tighter, picked up his pace and bent into the freezing gusts that lashed his face. Suddenly the skies opened and unleashed a torrential downpour. I looked up and saw a large crow flying alone in the wind, away from its flock, contrary to the custom of birds. What was it doing up at this time? The bird cawed several times, as though to warn of worse to come. Worshippers at the little mosque concluded their dawn prayers, repeating the final salutation of peace behind Sheikh Ragab, then left the small mosque grumbling under their breath or, perhaps, muttering prayers to their Lord to ward off the evil of the cawing crow.

Ramses, Nabawi, and I drove to the village. Ramses had insisted on coming while I had insisted for Nabawi to join. Now that Nabawi had grown accustomed to me and had come to trust me, he no longer took the evening trek into the village to spend the night. I only managed to persuade him to leave the grounds by assuring him I had my gun with me. Even then, he waited inside the safety of Ramses's hut until all the worshippers had left. He then made a dash for the car, jumped into the backseat, and concealed his face behind his kufiya.

The driver drove toward the main market where Umm Salib lived. The street was completely still. "Nobody here gets up before seven," Ramses explained, adding that most of the people in this quarter were Christian.

Three pairs of eyes had been deprived of sleep that night. One set was red, swollen, and anguished. The others were variously angry, worried, afraid, and lacking hope. Umm Salib was grieving the loss of her son while a neighbor tried to console her. The third woman was none other than Hoda Habib, who had appeared at the judges' lodge some months ago. She stood in the center of the room as still as a statue, staring into space with an alarmingly lifeless look. When she became conscious of our presence, she approached.

"This is Hoda, the Coptic woman, an eyewitness, sir," said the officer who had accompanied us. I winced inwardly at the epithet. When she recognized me, her face seemed to relax, or so I imagined. Still, she pretended not to know me, and I accepted that decision. She had changed considerably since I first saw her. Her body had filled out and, despite the dismal scene around us, she seemed to radiate contentment. I was about to ask the officer about other eyewitnesses before questioning her, but changed my mind, thinking most everyone else would probably have been asleep at the time of the murder, which I assumed had occurred within the previous hour or so. I signaled to Hoda to speak.

She related what she had seen up to the time when a man in the crowd outside the house called to Umm Salib to come out and see her son before he died. Sadly, fate was one step ahead. She spoke calmly, in a tone that was somehow soothing to the ear. After finishing her account, she fell silent, leaving me with the unpleasant task of asking her to accompany us.

We headed to the market to inspect the body. The moment we arrived, ululations and cheers rang out from the large crowd that had assembled there. They were for Hoda, whose chest started to heave from the emotion. I was so surprised, my mouth hung open despite myself. I turned to Ramses, who was directly behind me, and whispered,

"Why the hell are they cheering? Umm Salib's son is lying right there in a pool of blood."

"It's not about that, sir. It's because Madam Hoda is blessed. This is the first time in the history of the village that a Coptic house doesn't burn to the ground after a Molotov attack. The people here have been coming to her for her benediction ever since she arrived in the village.

I turned to Hoda. She was staring fixedly at the ground, face flushed. I gathered she didn't like being the center of so much attention. I asked her in a friendly tone, "So, what's this about you being a miracle worker?"

She scowled and before she could speak, Ramses put in, "It's a divine blessing, sir. She's protected by the Holy Virgin's love and mercy."

As there was nothing I could say to that, I turned to the crime scene. When I realized none of the people milling around had witnessed what happened, I had a sinking feeling. I then learned that the incident had occurred in broad daylight, yet no matter which officer I asked, I invariably received the same answer, word for word: "We'll inform you of their names within twenty-four hours."

Why did the police take so long to notify us of the crime? Why did they wake me at dawn and make it seem as though the murder had just occurred? This certainly gave somebody plenty of time to tamper with the crime scene if they wanted to. That mute witness will tell me nothing more than whatever they left there for me to see. Still, I had the police cordon off the scene, which I then divided into quadrants to help me proceed systematically. At the very least, I hoped I might be able to find proof of meddling. Evidently, they had combed the place very thoroughly.

I issued a summons for the person designated as Khalifa, requesting the police to conduct the initial inquiries. I handed the paper to the district police chief, who seemed about to doze off on his feet, judging by his loud yawns. As I turned to other business, the corner of my eye caught sight of the state security officer's hand swooping down like a vulture on a sleepy swallow in its nest to snatch the documents from the chief's hand and stuff them in his pocket. I said nothing.

I went over to Salib's prone corpse and stooped to inspect it. There were splotches of blood on his back and a long coagulated slash on his throat. I looked up to find a short man with ears like soup ladles next to me, smiling for no reason. He introduced himself as the medical examiner. This gave me some relief. I told him I had finished and that he could take the body to the morgue and perform the autopsy immediately.

"We've been standing out here in the middle of the street too long, sir," Nabawi whispered nervously in my ear the moment I stepped outside the yellow tape.

I patted the gun on my side, which made his anxious face relax a bit. I pointed to the large rifle slung over his shoulder, and said, "You have nothing to be afraid of."

He looked around to make sure no one was listening, then bent toward my ear again, "It isn't loaded, sir. It's just for show. But sir, I beg you, by the life of the Prophet, don't tell a soul."

I wasn't sure whether to feel sorry for him or sorry for us all. We all depend on others and need someone to have our backs. I gave Nabawi a smile. I wasn't sure what I meant by it, and left Nabawi to interpret it how he pleased.

With Nabawi crouched low in the back seat of the courthouse car, I followed the medical examiner and Salib's body to the district hospital. I cannot bear to watch an animal being slaughtered, nearly gag at the sight of blood, but now I had to examine a corpse. The thought of attending an autopsy filled me with horror.

We arranged ourselves around a wooden table in a dimly lit room. The smell was overwhelming. It conjured up the image of open graves, and made me feel I was in a dress rehearsal for the last resting place. Suddenly, Ramses stepped out of the shadows and took his place by my side. I wondered how he got to the morgue before us. He slowly scratched his scalp while he studied Salib's corpse, as though he were now a forensic expert. Behind him stood Nabawi, sweat pouring out of every pore despite the frigid temperature in the room. One might have thought he was the killer, judging by the rapid movement of his lips, his muttering of what seemed to be Quranic verses, despite the large cross tattooed on his wrist. I kept meaning to ask him about that, but somehow it slipped my mind whenever the opportunity arose.

Across from me, on the other side of the table, the medical examiner and his assistant got to work. The assistant opened a large leather medical bag with a latch that had grown loose from frequent use. He extracted the required instruments and set them on a tray with the concentration and zeal of an artist laying out his pens and brushes. The tools of the art here, though, were saws, an autopsy hammer, a large mallet with a leather head and worn wooden handle, and glass vials of diverse shapes and sizes. After the two men snapped on their surgical gloves, the assistant handed the scalpel to the medical examiner, who swiftly made a long and deep cut into Salib's abdomen. The red incision was as straight as a line drawn with a ruler on a blank piece of paper. My stomach lurched violently as the medical examiner extracted the bowels and set them aside. The assistant snipped off a length of intestine and inserted it into one of the beakers. The rest of us looked on as they continued their work amidst a tomblike silence.

Suddenly, a loud crash broke the silence. The medical examiner's hands trembled and his assistant jumped. I too felt a moment's panic. The only one who had remained unperturbed was Ramses. He was now on his knees, calmly tending to Nabawi, who had fainted and collapsed with all his weight onto an old wooden chair that shattered upon impact. After several failed attempts to bring him back, Ramses dragged Nabawi's body by his feet out of the room and handed him to the care of a police officer and some guards. He then resumed his place at the table as though nothing out of the ordinary had happened and nodded to the medical examiner to resume. I found it hard to suppress a smile as the doctor absorbed himself in his work again. Selecting one of the saws, he opened Salib's chest and spread the ribs, exposing the heart. The assistant reached in and extracted a portion of the lungs, which looked like a couple of large almonds, and placed them in a stainless steel dish. The examiner then flipped the body onto its stomach, wiped away the clotted blood, and examined the wound on Salib's back. He shot me a meaningful look.

I bent over to examine the wound and nodded my agreement to an opinion the examiner had no need to express. Our eyes met again, but this time he said nothing. He picked up a different saw and began to work on Salib's skull, sawing the bone layer after layer until he reached the cranial vault.

He gave Salib's brain a casual inspection and dictated some observations to the assistant, who jotted them down in a small notebook. I began to grow suspicious of the autopsy technique. It seemed crude, if not outright wrong. But who was I to say; I was no expert.

The medical examiner took a large magnifying glass from his pocket and examined Salib's other wounds. He handed me the lens. There were many small punctures in Salib's back. The doctor extracted some bullet fragments and placed them in a third bowl. With the assistant's help, he flipped the body onto its back and instructed the assistant to stitch it up.

My stomach lurched again as the assistant gathered up the intestines and other extracted pieces of Salib's body and piled them back into the stomach cavity as though hurriedly packing a suitcase. He took a long thick needle from his medical bag, reached to a spool on a nearby counter, and pulled off a length of what resembled the type of twine used to make burlap sacks. He drew the walls of the stomach together and fixed them in place with three large sutures. Ramsis handed him a white sheet he had found in a cabinet drawer in the far corner of the room. How would he have known that was where the sheets were kept? After the assistant covered Salib, Ramses leaned over the body's chest and recited some Biblical verses. We all turned to leave.

As I approached the door, the medical examiner took my elbow and held me back, then bent toward my ear to confirm my earlier suspicion.

"Salib was shot twice in the back. It was what caused him to fall. The bullets only wounded him, but the actual cause of death was severe hemorrhaging and a sudden drop in blood pressure after his neck was slashed from behind with a sharp instrument."

"So that means he was still alive as Hoda Habib testified, then someone came along later, attacked him with a knife, and ran?

"Yes. But it happened before she and the other witnesses came out of the house."

"I need a preliminary report stating that immediately, please. You can send the final report to my office later."

He led me down a corridor to a room to do as I had asked. On the way, I spotted the state security guy talking with Ramses, whose crafty smile seemed to play around his eyes.

13

THE BRANCHES OF THE TREES swayed like swings rocking gently in the breeze. The peacefulness was marred by the loud buzz of bees. I was staring blankly out the open window, resting my arms on the sill. A sudden gust of hot wind blew dust and sand into my face. I stood up, banged the window shut, moved to a remote corner of the spacious living room, and continued to wait for Farida to come down. The swaying branches cast broken shadows on the furniture and walls. They danced like impish spirits, taunting me and trying to goad me into leaving. Once again, I felt like a guest whose welcome had run out but whose host was at a loss for a polite way to get rid of him.

The buzzing continued to grate even though I had shut the window tightly. The air had turned yellow with the fine sand carried by the *khamasin* winds. I could still make out small swarms of bees, hovering over the vines that climbed the walls as though scrambling in vain to flee. I felt smothered in the oppressive silence inside the house, which was where Farida's family lived. A surge of anger at my situation increased my sense of solitude.

I stole a quick holiday in Cairo so I could help Farida do up the apartment that would become our conjugal home. Since my arrival, I had been going through the same routines: outings with people whom I realized bore no resemblance to me. Most of my conversations with them had nothing to do with who I was. Half of what I said lacked genuine affection and the rest was flattery verging on flagrant hypocrisy. Farida's conversations with her friends and their husbands were like choruses of croaking frogs. Or perhaps I had grown fond of the conversations of the real frogs I heard in Tayea every night.

I had little time to myself. She would ring every quarter of an hour to ask me versions of the same question: Which fabric, tile, furniture store offered me a discount as a member of the judiciary? Over and over again, I tried to make her understand that I was not entitled to such privileges and that if such offers did exist, they would be nothing less than veiled bribes paid upfront in exchange for services rendered later. No respectable judge would accept them, I stressed. Every time she would give the same reply,

"So how come Magdi can get everything for half price? He's a colleague of yours, isn't he? Isn't it your right to get things at discounted prices?"

I could only sigh and collapse on the nearest chair, defeated. There was no answer I could give to that silly question. I was not about to get into a discussion about her brother-in-law's character. What point was there in arguing with her anyway? I was going to marry her, come what may, because my life proceeded in one direction and I couldn't think of another route to take. Often I felt I wasn't at the steering wheel. I was in the passenger seat of a car called customs, traditions, and "this-is-how-things-are-done." This is how you get engaged, get married, plan a wedding, do up a flat, build a family, raise children, and so on. I might be asked for my opinion a few times along the way, but for the most part, the driver ignored me and fixed his eyes on the road ahead. That road was leading me to all those little things that were clamping me in one fetter after the other with every passing day, forcing me to remain silent when I should shout and to submit when I should resist. I'd become an actor assigned to play several different roles. I was constantly switching masks and costumes, depending on the scene and the audience. I'd mastered the art of changing so quickly and subtly that no one caught on. If my audience was large, it was also silent. It didn't applaud or boo or interact with me in any way. Maybe they were actors too. Maybe I was a member of their audience, and they were as impressed by my silence as I was by theirs.

Shortly before dawn, after another sleepless night, I texted Farida that I had to report back to work for an important case. The SMS spared me the protest I would face if I phoned her. I drove back to Tayea with uplifted spirits. I smiled and breathed a sigh of relief when I saw the faded blue sign announcing my arrival in the village. It was like coming home after a long absence.

By the time I reached the rest house, the morning sun shone well above the horizon. Nabawi was there to greet me. He saluted me and cried, "Welcome back, sir." I wondered if he was relieved I had returned earlier than planned. He must have felt I had the power to protect him from whatever unknown danger had been lying in wait for him for two years without ever revealing itself. I waved to him then went straight up to my bedroom and fell asleep with an inexplicable smile on my face.

I awoke late on Friday morning. I yawned lazily. I didn't want to leave my bed, so I flipped over onto my side and prepared to go back to sleep, hopefully until prayer time. I may or may not have drifted off, but my eyes shot open at the screech of the loudspeaker from the small mosque. The attendant had turned the volume up so high that it sounded like he was at the foot of my bed, shouting, "Hajj Mohammed Hambouli from al-Ezba al-Bahariya has passed to the mercy of God. The funerary service will be held in the mosque after Friday prayers. We are of God and to Him we shall return. In the name of God the Just and Merciful . . ."

His voice was thick and nasal like a chanter at a *zikr* ceremony. He repeated the announcement three times, chasing sleep from my eyes as effectively as a gunshot startles birds from a tree. Then came the grating voice of Sheikh Ragab, who recited some Quranic verses just as loudly. I climbed out of bed and went downstairs to prepare a light breakfast before heading to Friday prayers. Suddenly, I thought I heard footsteps in the house. This was Ramses's day off so I pricked up my ears.

On my first weekend here, Ramses had walked in while I was doing my ablutions before setting off for Friday prayers. He jumped back and stared at me as though he had seen a ghost. I had anticipated such a moment ever since he had asked me my full name and drawn the conclusion that I was Christian, but I had never expected such a strong reaction. Not that I said anything, of course. Six days later, he asked permission to change his weekly day off from Sundays to Fridays. Now he surprised me once again. He stood with that slick smile engraved on his face. My immediate inclination was to spoil his mood, so in an icy voice, I asked him why he had that smile pasted on his face all the time. I would never have expected his answer:

"Here in the village, sir, the smile is the secret of life. Have you ever seen a pharaonic statue with a frown?"

I stared at him until the phone rang. It was Brigadier General Hazem Amr from State Security Investigations. He wanted to meet me and was already on his way to the lodge. There was no way I could get out of it and I needed to have a word with him anyway. Ramses had gone to the kitchen to wash some dishes. I called him back to ask why he had come to work on his day off. This time it was his voice that was icy.

"Things have been tense since the fire at the church. All eyes are on Tayea these days."

Before I could respond, I found the SSI officer standing in the middle of the room. Ramses must have left the door open. Had that been prearranged? I became unusually apprehensive and suspicious.

The officer shook my hand warmly as though I were an old friend. This was an informal visit, he said as we took our seats. The purpose was to "steer the ship of investigations to a safe shore." I leaned back in my chair and crossed my legs as I waited for him to describe the features of that shore that he alone could see.

"Unfortunately, the witnesses are all telling conflicting stories, as you've seen from the investigations. As for this Khalifa guy, no one here knows who he is, and according to the investigations conducted by our department, no such person exists. In other words, we have no suspect."

"No, sir. Hoda Habib is an eyewitness and Umm Salib gave a description of him. Nabawi Dib, the guard at the lodge, told me he had seen him before and could identify him, and several of the stall owners in the market know his name. Maybe Khalifa's an alias, but—"

"No. We have no evidence of such an alias. Our investigations have been unable to produce a perp. We have no leads. This appears to be an isolated case, a dispute between villagers over crops or irrigation rights that spun out of control. You know, that kind of thing. Or maybe some guy went off his rocker, did something crazy and ran off. Anyway, I'll go speak with the district SSI director and see what he has to say. I'm sure we'll get an answer soon."

I set my feet down to emphasize my point. "Why is it that whenever a Copt gets killed in our country, it's always a cold case or a nutcase?"

The officer shifted so far forward that he nearly fell off. He caught himself in time, but had to stand up quickly to keep from losing his balance. Recovering his composure, he said,

"Believe me, Nader Bey, this has nothing to do with me. I have nothing to gain or lose. Most of the people here are Copts. It's in our interest to identify the killer, not to cover him up. As you know, most of the land here is owned by Muslims, and we have to protect their property. You could have given Judge Radwan the usufruct to that piece of land, but you only did what you thought was right and in keeping with the law. I'm doing what's right too, and according to the book."

I changed the subject so as not to get pulled in by the undertow of his twisted logic.

"What about the cross that someone keeps painting on Hoda Habib's house? Is that another unidentifiable perp?"

"Look, sir. That Coptic lady Hoda fraternizes with demons. She paints the crosses on her door herself in order to draw attention and attract customers. She reads their palms, tells them their horoscope, gives them a blessing—you know, the whole charlatan act. Our investigations have confirmed this. Our office has already sent you a memo informing you that she's an unreliable witness. We're looking into her right now, because she's not from around here. Or do you have another opinion?"

The officer took a gulp of water from the plastic bottle he was holding, then resumed without waiting to hear my answer.

"As for those other witnesses you questioned and who told you they saw nothing, they were telling the truth. It's not our job to pressure anyone. If we did, you'd be investigating us on charges of torture and coercion."

I sat back and crossed my legs again.

"Why do you let Sheikh Ragab keep ranting against them after prayers? And that's not to mention what he says in his Friday sermons."

"I'm a police officer, sir. Not a sheikh who interprets Quranic verses."

"So, let me know if I got this right. The assailant of Mohammed Alwan, who's Muslim, couldn't be identified and Salib's killer couldn't be identified either. So each side has an unidentifiable assailant working for them?"

"Those were ordinary criminal cases, sir. That's not my department. Of course, if the perp confessed, we'd have him standing before you first thing in the morning. As I said, sir, it's not in our interest to cover up for anyone."

Ramses entered the room, and we fell silent.

"The mayor's outside and asks if he can come in, sir." The question was addressed to me, but Ramses's eyes were pinned on the SSI officer. I told Ramses to ask the mayor to wait until Hazem and I finished our conversation, but the brigadier asked me to invite the mayor in, so I grudgingly agreed.

Ramses could not have taken more than two steps out of the room before the mayor entered, strutting like a crow. He went first to the officer and greeted him with a bow so deep I feared he would bump his head on the floor. Then he turned to me to offer me a salute like a semaphore, raising both palms as though to sound the call to prayer. Taking the seat nearest to the officer, he said, "Please, sir. Don't let the mayor's post go to anyone outside the Tayea family, sir."

He proceeded to relate to the officer the history of his grandfather and father and how they had preserved the stability of the village through the ages. Then he turned to me, as if suddenly remembering I was in the room in my capacity as host.

"Please, put in a good word for me, Nader Bey. The mayorship of this village has been in my family for fifty-three years. My grandfather's antique hand-crank phone is still hooked up in the mayor's residence. I'd die of grief if they cut the line."

I offered him a vague smile which he didn't see because he had turned back to the officer to plead, "Please don't have me transferred. You know I'll do anything for the minister of interior. You'll see, sir, in the next elections."

The officer placed one leg on top of the other so that the sole of his shoe faced the mayor, and curled his lips into a sneer. "And who did the Bishois vote for in the last elections? And what about the Samaan, Wassef, Abanoub, and the other Coptic families over on the west bank; who did they vote for? We'll speak about this and other details in my office. There's no need to pester me everywhere I go."

"I swear sir, we're on top of them at election time—all the way to the polling station. None of them would have voted the wrong way, sir, because that would be like betraying the bread we broke together."

"You should have made double sure while they were standing in line, before they went inside. You should have done as I told you and reminded them that a 'Yes' in the booth gets a 'Yes' outside it."

"But sir, I told Ramses to—"

"That's enough. We'll talk later. Drop by my office tonight."

"Yes, sir. And—"

The officer held up a hand to silence the mayor, who had clearly strayed from the script. From what Tayea let slip in front of me, it was clear that, to the SSI officer, Copts were no more than a large voting bloc.

The mayor backed out of the room, bowing repeatedly, alternately patting the top of his head and his chest with both hands to express his gratitude and heartfelt wishes for our well-being. He may have addressed us in the plural form, but his eyes were directed singularly at the brigadier.

It was a depressing scene, but at least I had satisfied my conscience. I had performed my duty within the scope of my profession. I rose to shake the officer's hand, thinking he would leave shamefacedly. Instead, he said that the main reason he had dropped by that day was because I had requested an inquiry into the land sales and purchases that occurred after the arson cases. State security had nothing to do with such matters, he said with an indifference that struck me as overplayed. If I wanted, I could pursue the matter with the Agricultural Cooperative Association. "The co-op has all the property registration ledgers. You can go look at them there. Let's save our inquiries for the serious things." He stood to shake my hand and continued, articulating each syllable, "I suggest you withdraw your request for an inquiry into a matter outside our jurisdiction. I thought I'd tell you this in an informal way, out of respect for the Office of the Public

Prosecution. It wouldn't be right to keep you waiting for a reply you'll never get."

The insolence was blatant, but I let it drop. I had nothing to gain from clashing with an SSI officer at this point. He would never budge from the "out of our jurisdiction" line even though he was the only player on the chessboard. No piece moved without his say-so. At least I was acting on my own free will when I opted to remain silent and keep playing. Just as the officer was about to cross the threshold, another thought occurred to me.

"Excuse me sir. I have just one more question, if you don't mind. How long do you think our 'Coptic brothers,' as you call them, will be confident and content with the cosmetic protection you give them?"

He flashed me a confident smile and said, "Just as confident and content as your guard Nabawi is with the protection you give him with that unloaded gun of yours. Or do you see things differently?"

We bounced around in the car as it threaded its way along narrow, bumpy roads between the fields. This was the shortcut we took to save time. My glasses slipped off onto my chest for the umpteenth time. I folded them and stuffed them in my pocket with a grunt. Without them, I neither see nor hear well.

At last, the car pulled up to the gate of the Azhari Institute. We had to pass through three security checkpoints along the way, so I was half an hour late. I bounded up the stairs to the polling station on the third floor. I'd been appointed as a member of the judicial commission supervising the second stage of the People's Assembly elections.

Two candidates were competing in this district. One was running for the ruling National Democratic Party, and the other was a Muslim Brotherhood candidate, which everyone knew though it wasn't stated openly. His campaign poster featured only a picture of a man with a trimmed beard in an elegant suit. He was probably banking on the successes the Muslim Brotherhood scored in some of the Delta governorates in the first round. Days earlier, he held a campaign rally in the little square in front of the largest church and pledged to support Copts as much as Muslims.

Girgis, the clerk, laid out the voter registration ledgers while I inspected the wooden ballot box to make sure it was empty, before setting it in front of me on the table. I was curious to see what symbols the candidates had chosen to represent themselves to illiterate voters. I took a peek at a blank ballot: the NDP candidate had chosen a crescent moon (an Islamic symbol) while the Muslim Brotherhood organization had chosen an airplane for its candidate. Nabawi, who'd accompanied me—willingly for a change—took up a position in a corner near the fabric screen that had been placed before the door. From where he sat, he would be able to see the people coming in without them seeing him. I caught sight of someone I didn't know in the room. In answer to my inquiring glare, he said he was the "mayor's delegate." I shooed him out with a flick of the wrist.

For over four hours, not a single voter appeared in my polling station. Just as the clock was about to strike five, I heard footsteps coming up the stairs. I nudged Girgis, who'd dozed off and pulled myself up. I knocked on the table twice to alert Nabawi, whose face was shrouded in a kufiya. He raised a hand, signaling he was still present and accounted for.

"Good afternoon! How are things going in the polling station? If you need anything, the police are here to serve you."

The SSI officer marched into the room in the company of the police chief, the head of police investigations, three police officers, and ten conscripts. This sizable military force made my polling station feel rather cramped. I stood up to greet them without concealing my annoyance, and added that the ballot box was still empty. All remained blank-faced except the officer, who laughed and said, "It's still early, sir. Don't count your chickens yet."

I answered with a weak smile and drew him by his elbow outside the room. I led him to the balcony off the corridor, overlooking the main street. It was as empty of voters as the ballot box was of votes. I took a step toward the officer and said,

"Tell me, honestly, where is everyone?"

"Your guess is as good as mine. When we get people to the polls, you guys cry foul. When they don't show up on their own, you say, 'Where is everybody?' There's just no pleasing you. So we stopped trying and washed our hands of this business. All is fair and square, as you can see."

"What I find hard to understand is that no one's showed up to vote for the Muslim Brotherhood candidate. Most of the registered voters here in the Azhari Institute are Muslim."

The officer shook his head and shrugged.

"Okay, then. Where are all the supporters for the NDP candidate?"

"Oh, come on, sir. It's not as though this one polling station's going to make him or break him. Stop worrying. The elections are free and fair—this time!"

He laughed. I didn't even smile. It wasn't funny.

Suddenly his walkie-talkie crackled, then came a voice barking orders to block off the side roads leading to the Azhari Institute.

I lifted my eyes from his walkie-talkie to meet his cold stare, and said, "Obstinacy breeds heresy."

"Heaven forbid, sir. May God protect us from the heretic. We've been notified that pro-Brotherhood demonstrations have started. There's always a risk that they can turn violent. That's why we blocked the roads. Our job is to protect public buildings and the people. And, of course, you, sir, before all others."

He left with his mini-force in his wake, apart from a single conscript—the kid may have been left behind by accident. From my position on the third floor, I watched the soldiers march out through the institute's forecourt. I was curious to see what they would do when they came to that large, old sycamore tree that partially blocked the gateway. The trunk was very thick and its roots stretched deep into the ground, though it no longer bore fruit. The soldiers had to slow down and step gingerly over the cracked pavement around it before proceeding on their way. The tree's copious branches provided excellent shade for the police vehicles parked beneath it. No other cars were allowed to park there. If the police vehicles left, some conscripts would drag over a metal barrier to reserve their place. For a fleeting second, I wished I could cut down the tree. Obviously, that would have been impossible; I was alone here.

I returned to the polling station where I found Girgis and Nabawi playing hear no evil, see no evil. I pulled out a book from my briefcase—Tawfiq al-Hakim's *Justice and Art*—and passed the time reading. At about six o'clock, the soldier posted outside the door poked his head around the screen to announce that some voters had arrived.

"At last!" I said as I sat up and smiled as brightly as a shop owner about to receive a customer who promised to fill his empty cash register. Girgis opened his ledger as the first two appeared. It was Rizq, the electrician from the church, and his wife, Hoda Habib. They nodded a silent greeting, seemingly too exhausted for more. After I pressed them, they explained that the police had ringed the area with checkpoints on all the roads leading to the institute. The first one was five kilometers away. They had to walk the whole way in order to cast their vote. Hundreds of people were held back. The police were checking ID cards and only letting non-Muslims through.

What could I say? Rizq went into the booth to vote while Hoda waited since she wasn't a registered voter in Tayea. After they left, a farmer called Naguib Samuel and his wife Ferial came in. They cast their votes and left after relating the same story.

At 7 p.m., I closed the polling station, signed the ledger, and put all the unused ballots in a large government issue envelope which I secured with a red wax seal. I couldn't control my curiosity. Before sealing the ballot box, I reached in and pulled out the few ballots in there and looked at them. A laugh escaped me, though it was closer to a snort. I refolded them and put them back in the box. Girgis fixed me with a questioning look, asking for an explanation. The ringing of my cell phone broke the silence. It was my boss inquiring how I was getting along.

"Praise the Lord, and He alone shall we praise whatever may befall us. I received a total of three ballots today. All for the Muslim Brotherhood candidate."

14

FATE WAS GENEROUS TO ME that evening. It dispelled the clouds of sorrow and despair, and let me bury Khidr in the deepest folds of my memory. The days of my life until then had seemed as many as the stars in the sky. Now I could begin my life anew, with the moon lighting my night with joyful candles, escorting me down the path of happiness. I made my way slowly so I wouldn't reach the end too soon.

The night was like no other, since Rizq melted my fears in his arms. He let me savor the pleasure tenderly, leisurely, and I pleaded with Ecstasy to hold off a little before surprising me with the final bliss. She did, gently holding the cup so I could sip the wine of life with a heady delight. Rizq's lips and mine met, joined in a single breath like the song of double-piped flute. Our souls embraced in a dreamlike dance, moving to the rhythm of our bodily symphony, mending the cracks and fissures in my wounded soul.

Rizq got up early the next morning. He had a full day ahead of him in a nearby province. The job was a long one, so he would have to spend a night or two there.

"But I'm afraid of sleeping alone in this huge bed," I jested as I slid out from under the covers.

"The bed's jinxed."

I was surprised by his curt answer, but I laughed and pretended to pout.

"But why?"

As he dressed, he explained that he had bought it twenty years ago from the church. It once belonged to the village mayor, who had sold it after redecorating his house. Long before that, it had belonged to the Khedive Said. It was his last sickbed, and he died in it, so his son, the Khedive Ismail, was afraid to sleep in it.

"Me, I spent half the nights of my life in this bed, unmarried. Now you've appeared in my life at last, and you haven't been able to get pregnant." He bowed his head and added, "I'm thinking of selling it. Maybe that will lift the curse, and we'll make a bit of money from it as well."

We said nothing more about the bed, and it seemed that the decision had already been taken. I did not feel anything either way. It wasn't as though my life had ever presented me with an array of alternatives from which I could pick the one I liked best. I'd never had a choice in anything. My father died before I finished secondary school. My mother then married a Muslim ten years younger than she was. She'd fallen in love with him. The rumor spread that she'd been having an affair with him while my father was still alive, so they fled to a faraway village which was majority Muslim. They dragged me along with them because, as my mother told me, "they would have killed us" if we'd stayed in the village I grew up in. Her husband wanted me from the moment he first set eyes on me. I tried to avoid him, his leers, his hints, his constant harassment. Eventually the hunter got his prey.

I wasn't even sixteen years old yet. My mother was afraid her husband would divorce her or take a second wife if she expressed outrage at what he did to me. Maybe he mattered to her for more than the sense of security he provided; it was impossible to say, but she certainly had nowhere else to go, having been disowned by her own family for marrying a Muslim.

Due to a lack of means, she enrolled me in the teachers' college instead of university. After obtaining my certificate, I was hired as an Arabic language teacher in the elementary school in my step-father's village. From day one, I could never muster up enthusiasm for my job. Part of the reason was the instructions handed down to us from the Ministry of Education every year so that the ministry could announce the same result at the end of the school year: "All the students passed; not a single fail."

I had a run in with the dean when I tried to make a change. He had me transferred to another school. It was in the same district but too far away to commute, so I stopped reporting to work and eventually they dismissed me. That gave me time to focus on my hobbies: keeping up my diary, writing poetry, and reading stories.

Whether it was because her husband no longer wanted to support me or because of what he had done to me, my mother had decided to cast me out of her life. When I turned twenty, she said it was time for me to marry. We fought, but I soon caved in. What a match she made: Khidr, the stable worker, and Hoda, the college graduate; a brute as ugly as sin with an evil heart, and me, a woman half his age who people compared to Shadia in both appearance and voice; Khidr, a man too stupid and mule-headed to ever do his job right, who thought himself the smartest man in the world, and me, the teacher; Khidr, the Muslim, and me, a Copt who would never change her faith.

Khidr was the only one who would accept a non-virgin, my mother said. As it turned out, I felt a trickle of red blood between my thighs on my first night with him, announcing too late that I was the victim of ignorance all along. I thought of filing a suit to annul my marriage, as there was no longer anything for him to hide or expose. The good Lord had actually protected my honor after all.

Every night, he submitted me to a long, hellish ordeal. He was like a freight train focused only on its last stop, tearing through every station along the way with indifference. Reaching that last stop, he discharged his cargo as though it was too heavy a burden to bear and emitted a long deafening whistle. Looking back, I felt certain that Christ kept me from bearing Khidr a child for a reason. Our Lord wants the best for us, and I could not believe that Khidr's seed would ever bring good.

I left Nader Bey's office after giving my statement. I felt comforted, though it would be hard to explain why. Maybe it was because he believed me even though everyone else's testimony contradicted mine, making me look like a liar. They even tried to claim that Khalifa did not exist, although I was able to describe him. When confronted, they said he might have been the person who called out to Umm Salib to urge her not to resist. He was only looking out after her well-being, they said. He even invited her to come out to see her son before he breathed his last breath.

At first, when Nader Bey confronted me with the other witnesses, it made me feel as though I was the one accused of murdering Salib. Images of Khidr's death flashed to mind. I'd be in exactly the same situation. Probably the same types of witnesses would say they saw me kill him. The very thought made me tremble. At every word I told the prosecutor, the other witnesses rolled their eyes, clicked their tongues, shook their heads, and stared at me in fake amazement. I began to feel I had lost my mind.

Just before I left Nader Bey's office, the large ledger on his desk caught my attention. Nader Bey noticed and asked me to explain. At first I said it was nothing, but he pressed me. I said I had seen one just like it in Ramses's hut at the judge's rest house on my first night in Tayea.

"What does the "A" on the cover mean, sir?"

He answered with a broad grin. It was as though he already knew I had seen the ledger and merely wanted to hear me confirm it. When he noticed me growing nervous again, he asked me to take a seat and ordered me a tea to calm me down. Then he had me recount in detail everything I recalled about that mysterious ledger, whose significance he was unwilling to explain to me, and he recorded every word I said.

If only the judge who heard my suit to divorce Khidr had Nader's perspicacity. If he had been someone like this public prosecutor, I would not have ended up killing a man. I had prayed for a way to get an annulment from my first day of marriage and, in the end, sought a divorce. My mother, whose greatest fear was that her husband would divorce her, said I was like someone counting the days until his death. To me at the time, death seemed like a deliverance.

After a year of torment with Khidr, I asked him for divorce. Not only did he refuse, he became more violent. He beat me savagely more times than I could count. I filed for divorce on the grounds of physical abuse. He brought in a string of witnesses who testified to how kindly he treated me and that the branding iron he used to scorch me had fallen on my leg by accident. Khidr himself cried and begged the judge to believe him. He gave such a moving performance, I nearly believed him myself.

The case dragged on for a year, at which point the judge issued his verdict. He cautioned me against the "folly of divorce" as though he wanted to spare me from expulsion from paradise. Then he recited Quranic verses exhorting the faithful against the bane of divorce even if it was permissible. The judge was determined to apply the laws of sharia even though he was fully aware that his personal and scriptural bias meant he could not treat me, as a Copt, fairly. He sentenced me, my womanhood, and humanity to further death and dismissed my suit as though it were the work of some renegade.

I felt like screaming right there in the courtroom: I can't bear my life! Why can't you let me live in peace? You pass your judgement in the name of God, but He would never approve of what you're doing. Let me live according to my faith. God will judge me on the Day of Judgement, not you or Khidr. But I was too cowardly to say any of this.

When I emerged from Nader Bey's office, my mind preoccupied with all this, my thoughts turned so dark they nearly shook my faith in the power of the Cross. I decided to walk the whole way home to get a grip on my feelings. After a half-hour's walk, I spotted a long line of girls. The eldest could not have been more than sixteen years old. Many had not reached adolescence yet, though all wore head coverings and were heavily made-up.

Off to one side was an old man asleep in a wheelchair that seemed to have been hastily parked and forgotten. His head was tilted to his chest, a long stream of saliva dripping from the corner of his mouth. An aged woman tended to him, muttering her grievances into the air. Nearby, several men and women sat on the trunk of a fallen palm tree. Their patience was running thin, judging from their grumblings as they watched the snake-like line that seemed not to move. It began at the door of a lawyer known for his expertise in divorce and alimony cases. At the tail end was a young girl in tears. Her mother tried to buck her up while her father slapped her if she cried too loud.

I knew the girl. I had tutored her in Arabic to help her pass her exams and she came to my wedding reception. I went over to comfort her. She melted into my arms as though she wanted to hide inside me for protection. Her father wrenched her away so roughly that I feared he might have pulled her arm out of its socket. He narrowed his eyes at me, muttered something about the devil, and turned his back to me. What was she doing in this line? Was he going to marry her off at this early age? Or had he done that already and was now getting her divorced? I found it hard to believe that this man who had entrusted his daughter to me to help her succeed in school now tore her away from me to send her to a life with no future.

Sheikh Ragab was up ahead, keeping the line in order and handing out smiles to the girls. I spotted a neighbor of mine and went over to her in the hope she could clear up the mystery of what this line was for, but I ended up more baffled. All these girls were waiting to be presented to an elderly man from the Gulf who was visiting our village in search of a wife. The lawyer was taking care of the details. The parents of the selected bride would be awarded twenty thousand pounds. The child, herself, would be packed off to the Gulf along with the rest of the rich man's belongings, to spend a few months with him until he grew tired of her. Then he would divorce her, ship her back to Tayea along with some suitcases full of gifts, so she could marry for real.

I joined the clumps of parents with other onlookers as I contemplated the girls' faces. The anxious, far away look on one face told me she was worried about what would happen to her on her wedding night. Another looked nervously back and forth at the candidates in front and behind her in the meandering line. Was she hoping she'd be chosen over all the others? A third girl was hunched in a miserable slouch. She probably missed her friends with whom she would normally be playing in the fields at this time before sunset. She was being deprived of her childhood today and perhaps forever.

Then a vivacious girl caught my attention. She was laughing and chatting with others, seemingly indifferent to what lay ahead. Her burgeoning womanhood gave her an advantage over her dazed companions and, aware of it, she flaunted her charms, certain of her success, if that is what it could be called. Success at becoming a slave girl, at accruing more chains, tightened until they squeezed out all desire, killed her spirit, and turned her into human rubble.

I turned to a fifth girl, but they all had begun to merge into one another by then. I noticed an empty space in the line and felt for a moment that the space was for me. It seemed to beckon, to whisper, "Your turn has come again, Hoda. This banquet table of degradation still has servings of agony and grief for you."

Somehow, I envied the girls. Their lot was better than mine had been because at least their term was limited: a month or two in lockup in the arms of some rich Gulf Arab.

I'd been given a life sentence until I'd killed in self-defense and fled, and now the hangman's noose hung over my head.

I turned away from that wretched line before it could drag me deeper into despair over my lost youth. I could not shake off that heavy cloud of sorrow that turned everything around me into shades of gray, closing in around me and trapping me behind invisible bars. Try as I might, I could not escape. I was a permanent prisoner in my reality. My sole respite was with Rizq.

A flock of crows circled over the crowd, deaf, dumb, and blind to truth and justice. As I turned to leave, the cawing grew louder. Black wings spread wide, the crows formed larger circles and sailed closer, eyeing us hungrily. My feet grew heavier as I was overcome by an eerie sense that they saw us for what we ultimately were: delicious cadavers, nothing more.

Suddenly the weather shifted. Scattered rain gave way to heavy clouds that loomed until only feeble rays of sunlight peeked through the darkening horizon. Gusts of cold wind warned of the oncoming storm. The darkening skies stole an hour of daytime and the sun, frustrated and dejected, set early.

In the distance, I spotted Hilal tightening his kufiya around his head. He waved and signaled for me to wait as he broke into a run. My feet felt weighed down with sand bags, as I stood confused and terrified. I was sure he was bent on revenge for his brother's death. He was getting closer. Nothing stood in his way: he could take my life and rob me of Rizq. "Dear Jesus," I cried out. "With you and your blessing we begin our day. We surrender our will to you. Protect us and bless our souls. We see not your hand, but we have faith it supports us. In you we trust forever . . ."

15

I SUBMITTED A FORMAL LETTER excusing myself from election supervision duty. I pleaded that lumbar pain prevented me from sitting for long hours staring at the ballot box. I returned to work the following day and subpoenaed the director of the Agricultural Cooperative Society together with the village property registration ledgers. I had plenty of cases that warranted this subpoena, but I was looking for something unrelated to them.

Around noon, the ACS director was ushered into my office. He lay the ledgers open on my desk, all the same dark olive green and with a big "A" on the cover. He stepped back and stood with his hands folded in front of him. I ignored him.

The "A," I knew, stood for agricultural property holdings. Mohammed Ali, the Ottoman Viceroy of Egypt in the nineteenth century, had assigned that letter when he created the property register system two centuries earlier. This designation was kept for all the ledgers that had accumulated since.

I ran my finger down the columns, page after page, looking for certain lot numbers and their current owners. After a while, the ACS director cleared his throat, disrupting my concentration.

"If you could tell me what you're looking for, sir, I could find it for you in seconds," he said.

"You're missing a ledger," I replied without looking up.

"It went missing two years ago. We conducted a thorough inventory, but couldn't find it. We've been trying to square the missing properties with their current owners, but without the chains of title."

I narrowed my eyes at him, then picked up his ID card, which Girgis had placed on my desk before ushering the director in. His full name was Atef Nathan, a Coptic name. That meant that any question I asked would first have to pass through Ramses's filter before I received an answer the next day. I pressed the buzzer with a deliberate show of annoyance. Sergeant Ibrahim entered with his customary salute and click of his heels.

"Sir!" he barked.

"Take this man outside and have him wait in the corridor. And don't let him out of your sight."

That would keep Atef sweating for a while, I thought. The ACS director, stunned by my gruff treatment, surrendered to the sergeant. Keen to impress me, Ibrahim gave his charge a shove in the back to usher him out.

Returning to the ledgers, I soon detected a pattern. All the houses that burned down or whose owners had died during the past few years were bought up by members of the Bishoi clan. They also bought the small plots of agricultural land around the houses through the church. These plots were then sold to unknown Muslims from other villages both near and far, only to be resold to Copts soon after, with the result that the land ended up in the hands of the Bishois again.

I was looking at long and circuitous trails of fake sales and purchases. Of course, every single one of the intermediaries

—Copts and Muslims alike—would swear the transaction was legitimate and that they paid or received payment in full. If the Coptic holdings in the village increased overall, who was behind it? I would get no answer to that question, not even unofficially. That much I knew.

I drew up a list of all the plots of land sold within the past three years and closed the ledgers after making some ticks next to those who had nothing to do with what I was after and everything to do with putting Atef Nathan on the wrong scent. Towards this end, I opened the ledger listing properties belonging to the mayor and his relatives, and made a mark faintly resembling a cross next to some entries.

Then I picked up my list and studied it, trying to connect the dots. I had Sergeant Ismail bring Atef Nathan back in. He was visibly quaking. I told him I'd received numerous complaints about him, and paused to watch his eyes widen. I then added that I wouldn't act on them since he seemed like a decent person and his bookkeeping was in order. His face relaxed and he started to thank me profusely. I held up a hand to silence him, and told him to leave and take his books with him. I rested my hand on one, indicating he should leave it with me. Before he left, I instructed him to return the next day with the district's cadastral map. As he scurried out, as though afraid I might change my mind, I folded my list and inserted it in my wallet.

I looked up at the sound of three soft raps on my office door. Girgis entered, carrying a stack of documents bound by twine, and headed to the tall metal cabinet where we filed away closed investigations.

"What do you have there?" I asked.

"The case of Judge Radwan's land claim."

That surprised me because Mahmoud Bey had taken the case away from me.

"Why is it being filed among my cases when it was given to someone else?"

"But it wasn't." He explained that the case file had been sitting in my boss's desk drawer ever since I issued my ruling in favor of the Bishois. As to why, he said, "Judge Radwan files a lot of complaints. Mahmoud Bey, the district public prosecutor, holds on to them until the period for acting on them expires. He then calls me into his office and tells me to file them away, which I do, since my job is to obey."

I had Girgis set the bundle on my desk and undo the twine. Leafing through the contents, I came across my ruling to keep the status of the plot of land unchanged. No further action had been taken, meaning that ruling still stood. I got up and went to my boss's office, my mind whirling. Why had he taken the case from me and given me that lecture and then taken no further action?

"You made the right decision. Why should I change it?" he answered coolly. "It's your timing that was wrong. I told you to grant Radwan a provisional usufruct. That was to shut him up. We were going to revoke it later when things calmed down, but then you acted on impulse, and forced us to take a different course. I was as zealous as you when I was younger, but—"

He swallowed the rest of his sentence. After I pressed him to continue, he gave an exasperated sigh and said,

"You were right. So let's just say we learned a lesson here. Now, onto something important. There's a hearing downstairs I want you to attend. Make sure to take your sash with you." He contemplated me for a second, then added, "It's a good thing you're wearing a dark suit. The misdemeanors judge is quite a stickler for rules"

Just as I reached the door to his office, I turned to ask whether he could help me find bullets for my gun. Neither Ramses nor the mayor had any luck on that score. I saw a glimmer in my boss's eyes. He smiled as he opened a drawer and took out a silver gun, a recent model. Displaying it to me from all angles, he proceeded to give me a rundown on its specs and capabilities. I doubted that he spoke at such length about any of his legal cases. He asked me what kind of gun I had, as he pulled the slide on the barrel back and released it several times, delighting in the click-clack sound it made.

I took my gun from its holster and set it on his desk, embarrassed. Mine was small compared to his. It had a shiny black metal body with a wooden grip and a revolving cylinder that held only six bullets.

He gave a hoot of laughter as he picked up my gun, flipped it over, and weighed it in his hand.

"I hope you aren't hiding this from the Antiquities Authorities," he quipped.

I smiled faintly, and told him I'd inherited the gun from my father, who had probably inherited it from his father.

"You should donate it to a museum. You'd be performing a public service. They stopped manufacturing it twenty years ago. You'll never find bullets for it today."

He paused to take another look at it.

"Still, it could be of some use to you."

"How can it be of any use to me without bullets?"

"Think of it as a glass billy club. Anyone who sees it from afar will be very careful. But never threaten anyone with it up-close. That would really come back to bite you."

"All rise!" shouted the bailiff, needlessly stamping his foot on the ground.

Everyone stood up, eyes riveted on the door through which we entered the courtroom. All hoped that this was the door to vindication and succor. The judge and I, sporting our official sashes, strode into the room, followed by the court stenographer. Once we took our places, the judge broke the anticipatory silence in a business-like manner: "The court is in session."

I had to stifle my yawns during the misdemeanor proceedings. When each new case was called, I had to stand up and repeat the same phrase: "The prosecution requests the implementation of the articles of indictment." It sounded like a recorded message and undermined the stature of my office. Not that anyone in the room was interested in what I said; no one even looked in my direction. The center of attention was the judge. Everyone listened to the attorneys' pleas and arguments, then eyes riveted on the judge's lips as he pronounced the verdicts, half of which were acquittals. My pitiful regurgitations made no difference either way.

As I bobbed up and down, I noticed that the judge never looked at me. I gradually grew lazier, lowering my voice to a near mumble and rising only halfway out of my seat. My mind strayed to the murders and arsons that I was investigating, all cases that inevitably went cold. Even though I was only half focused on the proceedings, it filtered through that the last ten cases were all the same: on such and such a day, of such and such a month, in the year X, defendant Y planted onions in breach of the law. The defense lawyers pleaded for an acquittal. Some held that it was such a petty offense, while others argued that the law on onion cultivation was unconstitutional.

In each of these cases, the judge cast me a meaningful look that I was at a loss to interpret. Was he asking me to jog his memory? If so, I could be of no help. I had never even heard of that crime before. In fact, I was unfamiliar with all the cases on the docket that day. The district public prosecutor had referred them to the court and told me to attend as a representative of the Office of the Prosecution. I did as I was instructed.

The judge searched through the ten cases for the clue I had failed to provide. His frown betrayed his lack of success. He decided to rehear each of the ten cases, interrogating each suspect in turn, having each of them describe the "incident" in detail. He asked the same questions over and over, and the substance of the answers never varied.

"Did you plant onions in your field?"

"Yes, Your Honor. I've planted onions for as long as I can remember. My father and grandfather planted them as well."

"Just answer the question, yes or no."

"Yes, Your Honor, I planted onions."

"But that's against the law. What do you have to say?"

"What law? Is there an onion law? Well I'll be—"

"Quiet. Don't speak about the law. Only your lawyer is to do that. The charge here says you broke the law. What's your defense?"

"Your Honor, I don't know how to read or write. I just plant crops like other farmers."

The judge had the men taken back to the defendants' cage and called for a recess. As the judge and I left the room, the ten onion planters were escorted back to detention.

In the deliberation room, the judge said, as though talking to himself:

"All those cases have to be ruled on today."

I nodded.

"There's a mix, but I've noticed quite a few illegal onion-planting cases today. What do you think?"

"Yes, sir. There are."

"They're pretty new to me. I haven't seen many of them before in court."

"I'm new here myself, sir."

He looked at me from above his thick-lensed glasses and narrowed his eyes as though he thought I was evading the question or pulling his leg.

I tried to excuse myself, telling him I would be back for the sentencing. He slowly shook his weary head.

"It's a shame, really. Locking up the poor farmers just for planting onions."

I felt a lump in my throat, just picturing those unfortunate men as they heard the judge sentence them to prison just for farming like they and their ancestors have farmed all their lives. I suggested to the judge that maybe there was a flaw in the indictment and that we could reexamine the law on the cultivation cycle. He had already thought of that, he said, but he was unable to find a copy of the law in the courthouse library. All he had was the law number, a description of the charges, and the articles of indictment as recorded in the prosecutors' logbooks. Those contained summaries of the laws, statutes, limitations, offenses, and penalties, primarily so that they had this information on hand for the types of cases dealt with most frequently, as appeared to be the case with the onion-planting violation.

"I'm thinking about granting a continuance for a week so that I can study this more thoroughly."

"If you like, I can ask the district public prosecutor about this law. He's the one who referred the defendants to trial, so he must have a copy of it."

The judge's face lit up at this glimmer of hope.

I raced up to my boss's office on the second floor, related our predicament, and asked for a copy of the agricultural cycle law so the judge could have a look at it and make sure he was doing the right thing.

My boss leaned back in his seat with an enigmatic smile. He reached for a cigarette and lit it, then said calmly,

"I've been using my logbook for that violation for over ten years. It's one of those charges that have been handed down to us, generation after generation. Don't worry, the law exists and the charge is correct. I just don't have the actual text of the law itself."

"But what about those poor farmers getting locked up just for planting onions?"

"Who said anything about locking them up? A fine will do. Fifty pounds. The revenue goes to the agricultural co-op to buy seeds and fertilizers for them. Let them pay for the service. As they say, 'If they want a rope, make it from the hairs of their beards.'"

Although the compromise came as a relief and I thought the judge would feel the same, I was still uneasy about it.

"But that's a huge fine. It isn't just."

"What's unjust about it? Justice is equality in the dispensation of penalties. Our department charged those people in accordance with a law passed by the People's Assembly. The prosecution's job stops at referring defendants to court. We just bring the charges. The verdict is up to the judge."

16

HARDLY A WEEK WENT BY without another murder, a field vandalized, a cow poisoned, or a house set on fire. Never was a suspect produced, and I was constantly kept in the dark. The police in this village apparently thought justice amounted to equality in the dispensation of injustice. The villagers were racing each other to the police station to file complaints against their neighbors. But as soon as they were brought before me or a judge, they retracted their accusations. I could spend the rest of my life enumerating the ills of this village and never reach an end. I had embarked on a labyrinthine search for truth and justice, but I felt my goals and myself gradually fading. I feared turning into a zombie who obeyed without thinking, and so I applied for a transfer.

I read over my application for the third time, then signed it and headed to my boss's office. Dozens of people were outside his closed door in front of which stood a mean-spirited guard, his feet firmly planted in place. His unyielding frame, dark scowl, curt responses, and gruff commands could drive the stoutest citizen to despair and abandon all thought of filing a complaint.

I edged around the guard and entered a packed room. Mahmoud Bey's desk was strewn with files, many with their contents spilling out. The black office phone to his left was ringing off the hook. His ancient computer, long unused, served as an extra shelf. He seemed troubled. Despite the cold outside, the window was open to let out the smoke from his cigarette, which never left his lips. The window overlooked a small yard that kids from the nearby school used as their football field as of 4:00 p.m. every day, startling us whenever they cried "Goal!"

After a moment, I set my resignation letter on his desk where he could see it. I looked up at the picture of President Hosni Mubarak in a cheap gilt frame on the wall behind my boss. I shifted my gaze between Mubarak and my boss. He was listening to some of my colleagues who had conducted the preliminary investigations into the arson attack at the church. Then, to my surprise, he picked up my transfer application, folded it and said,

"Take a seat, Nader Bey. I'd like to have a word with you in private."

He cleared the room. I was sure he was going to reprimand me, especially when he tore my letter into tiny pieces and tossed it into the wastepaper basket. That troubled look returned to his eyes. After exhaling a thick cloud of smoke that he had built up in his chest, he calmly said,

"You can't just up and leave us after only five months. I need you here for a while yet. I know you're within your rights but you should also know my hands are tied by strict laws and conventions."

"I can't work this way. I feel I'm a performer in rehash after rehash of the same silly play with a director from another planet. He's not like us at all. He thinks completely differently. He doesn't give a hoot about justice and the rule of law. All he cares about is politics. If only he got that right. I appreciate the circumstances in the country right now, but I also know that most of the audience isn't cheering for us. They applaud that director, not because they're convinced by what he has to say, but because they're scared of him. I want—"

My boss pressed a bell that was so loud it shut me up. When his secretary appeared at the door, he said,

"Fetch me the coroner's report on Mohammed Alwan, the peacock guard."

He sat back, crossed his legs and fidgeted impatiently. I thought I was in for another lecture about the nature of our job and our code of conduct, and began to wish I hadn't spoken so openly. When the secretary returned with the file, Mahmoud set his feet down, shoved the file in my direction, and began to explain,

"As you may have heard, the prosecution ordered the exhumation of Alwan's body and the medical examiner confirmed that Alwan had been strangled to death, before his killer, or killers, set fire to the body and threw it off the roof of his house to make it look like suicide."

"Is there a suspect?" I asked, already knowing the answer.

"Not yet. But the Muslims are convinced the Christians did it."

I spoke a bit about who stood to gain from Alwan's death. Then we both fell silent.

"Believe me," he said after a moment, "Together we can get to the truth. There are fanatics on both sides. Even if we can't find out who the killer is right away, at least we can investigate this case and, if we run out of time, others can pick up wherever we leave off. Justice will be served in the long run, as long as we keep striving for it."

This pep talk encouraged me and I did feel I had a lead. I told him of my suspicions about Ramses and the agricultural holdings ledger hidden in his cabin. That was where we would find hard evidence on who gained from the sale of burned houses and fields after their owners were killed. My boss thought for a moment, then said that he had asked the district state security director to reopen the investigation into Salib's murder. Despite all attempts to cover up evidence and bury the case, the medical examiner's report found that Salib's throat had been slit after being shot.

"We have to find that so-called Khalifa," he said, looking at me earnestly, "The witnesses all say that he's the killer. And there's another Khalifa we have to find now that we know that Alwan did not die by suicide."

I pictured the scales righting themselves in the hands of Lady Justice, and smiled. Maybe there was hope. Reminding him of the property ledger that Ramses had, I offered to question him. My boss put another cigarette in his mouth, lit it from the previous one, and exhaled a large puff of smoke. He then issued a warrant to have Ramses arrested and his cabin searched, citing Hoda Habib's deposition to me regarding the ledger she had seen in Ramses's cabin.

With a fresh burst of energy, I stood up, eager to get back to work and ready to put aside the problems that had brought me to my boss's office to begin with. He stood too and gave me a hearty pat on the shoulder and a meek smile that I took as an apology for his previous behavior. I answered with a bright smile, signaling that I'd accepted the apology.

I set off with an assistant police detective and a small force from the police department. By way of camouflage and so that no one tipped Ramses off, I told them we had been

130

assigned to perform a land inspection to the west of the village. On the way, I told the driver to pass by my place, saying I had forgotten some important papers. Ramses was sitting on the steps of the veranda, feeding the dog that frequented the lodge. Nabawi Dib was holding a bunch of sugarcane reeds and next to him was a small pile of discarded remains from which he'd sucked out the sweet juice. I smiled to myself and thought, we're about to ruin that cozy setting. I got out of the car and walked to a point about midway between the lodge and Ramses' cabin.

Ramses stood up and approached me hesitantly. He looked anxious. He didn't have a clue what was happening. Then his head shot around as the police jumped out of the van and moved into formation like an army of ants. It hadn't sunk in yet that he was the lump of sugar they were after. I turned to the police force, calmly pointed at the stunned Ramses, and said,

"Arrest the suspect."

Ramses turned this way and that as though about to bolt, but he quickly got control of himself and shot me a defiant look. I was struck by the speed with which he rallied; I had begun to think he could no longer surprise me. Once the police cuffed him, I grabbed hold of his elbow and roughly led him toward his cabin. As we approached his door, he whispered that I'd lost him forever. I responded to him with an exact replica of his trademark grin.

We turned his cabin inside out. There wasn't a hole in a knot of wood that we left unexamined. I was ready to remove the boards on the facade of the cabin when we couldn't find the ledger inside. After a two-and-a-half-hour search, I turned to Ramses. He stood, relaxed, leaning comfortably against his door. His face had recuperated his greasy smile in full, leaving a sullen, frustrated frown on mine.

Hoda Habib's statements in the investigations helped persuade the district prosecutor to hold Ramses for four days in precautionary detention despite our inability to find the ledger. For me, the most pressing question now was how Ramses had, in fact, learned of the search. I presented the puzzle to my boss, who was just as flummoxed as I was. He said that he had told no one about the search, not even his secretary. We sat silently, slowly replaying the events in our minds as we tried to put the pieces together.

Then, almost simultaneously, we recalled our phone call as I bounded down the stairs of the public prosecutor's building to join the police and serve the warrant on Ramses. We had discussed the details of the plan. My boss held a finger to his lips to silence me as he directed a bitter smile towards our mobile phones on his desk.

After being taken into custody, Ramses remained as impervious as a statue. He said not a word of any significance to my colleague, who took over the investigation from me. He denied all knowledge of a ledger and any information about agricultural holdings. When confronted with the eyewitness testimony of Hoda Habib, he didn't flinch. To my greater amazement, I learned he denied even knowing her, saying she was a newcomer to the village. At that point, I knew they would not extend his detention. He would be released, the missing ledger would vanish forever, and this case would join all the others that were filed away as "unsolved."

I yawned and turned to go inside the lodge and catch up on some sleep. My foot struck a small, smooth stone.

Without thinking, I picked it up and hurled it towards the dense clump of shrubbery at the edge of the garden. A dog yelped, emerged from the shrubbery, and started to circle Ramses's empty cabin. It seemed I had accidentally hit the dog. It spun around, trying to lick its behind and make sure it was unharmed. After several unsuccessful attempts, it pranced off, happily wagging its tail.

Ramses was still in detention for the stipulated four days pending investigations. The red tape meant that he would be released a day later. The dog must have come for his daily meal and gone away hungry. I felt sorry for it. Rather than feed it another stone, I prepared a hearty meal from some lamb bones, the meat from which had settled in my belly the previous day, on top of which I poured some leftover broth. I set the bowl down near the dog. He sniffed at the meal, then bounded back to the cabin wagging its tail. He then returned to the meal only to sniff it and leave it again. I figured he was afraid of me, so I hid behind the open shutter that overlooked the veranda and watched. Once again, the dog approached the food and rejected it. Suddenly he pricked up its ears and ran up to the door of the cabin and began to scratch at it and bark.

I thumped my forehead with my fist. How blind I was. I hadn't read the signs right before my eyes. I leaped off the veranda, ran to the cabin, picking up a stone along the way, and smashed the window. Then, in a single gesture, I reached in to open the latch and sweep the curtain aside, revealing what I had at last suspected. Ramses was sitting on his bed, in his civilian clothing, eyes wide in alarm at the sight of me at his window. The dog was still barking.

17

A SPEEDING TAXI THUMPED ITS horn. Hilal, on the other side of the street, leaped out of the way before the car could hit him. He stumbled backward and fell. Before I knew it, I had latched onto the side of the open door of a passing minibus. The driver's helper grabbed my other hand and pulled me inside as the driver took off. This was the second time a heaven-sent escape route had arrived just in time to rescue me. How long could such luck hold out?

I silently recited the Lord's Prayer, "Our Father who art in Heaven . . . Forgive us our trespasses as we forgive those who trespass against us . . ."

I repeated the verses as quickly as I could in the hope that the words would outpace the tears that were welling in my eyes and stop them from flowing down my cheeks. I couldn't bear the thought of seeing Hilal for a third time. I began to pray out loud

". . . Lead us not into temptation, but deliver us from evil . . ."

When I looked back, I saw Hilal staring after the bus as he wiped the dust off his galabiya. People had gathered around him to make sure he wasn't hurt. I wondered whether he mentioned something to them about me. The cold Upper Egyptian wind forced us to close the windows, and the passengers' breath soon fogged up the glass of the rear window, concealing him from my view.

Next to me was a young girl with her mother. She turned around to kneel on the back seat and used her fingertip to trace a large heart on the window. With the flat of her hand, she wiped away the mist inside the outline. I smiled at her and together we peered through that portal. Hilal was gone.

I returned home exhausted. I could not shake that uneasy feeling that had clung to me all day. Maybe it was due to lack of sleep, or perhaps to the strain of having to deal with the village women's constant demands for my "benison." I sometimes wondered whether their brains were in their ears because they believed everything they heard. Whenever they had a problem, they brought it to the "Coptic woman's house" because they heard I would cure it. Women who couldn't bear children thought I had the power to make them fertile. It never struck them that I hadn't been able to bear children myself so far.

I was plagued by nightmares for several days straight. Not only had Hilal emerged from my past, he haunted my dreams. I felt leaden as I stared blankly through the bedroom window. I spotted a little bird hopping daintily from branch to branch on a tree. It seemed so carefree, until something scared it away. At least it could still fly.

"We're late Hoda. Let's go. Get a move on."

Rizq was waiting impatiently for me at the front door. I hastily collected myself and caught up with him. After a while, we were on a bench in the long corridor outside the office of the deputy public prosecutor, waiting to be given permission to enter. The waiting dragged on. People went in and came out, some looking comforted, others anxious.

Suddenly Sheikh Ragab's bilious face appeared in the corridor. He was followed by Saleh, the caretaker, who looked at me malignantly as he played with his moustache. The sheikh spat on the ground after he passed us. Feeling Rizq tense up, I grabbed hold of his hand tightly. He calmed down and gave my hand a gentle squeeze in return, but a short stream of expletives escaped his lips in a low voice.

Sheikh Ragab slipped some money to the soldier standing guard at the prosecutor's door and went inside without waiting for permission. This time, Rizq raised his voice, protesting against people who cut in line. Nader Bey called out to his guard asking what the noise was about. A second later we were ushered into the large room where the sheikh was explaining his cause. As we took a couple of seats in the corner, the sheikh protested our presence. Nader Bey insisted we stay and told the sheikh to continue.

"May Allah give me strength," grumbled Sheikh Ragab. He quickly put on an ingratiating smile and intoned, "In the name of God the Just and Merciful . . . Some time ago—this was before you arrived, sir—a Copt from the village received the guidance of the Lord and converted to Islam—"

Rizq coughed loudly and cleared his throat. Nader Bey shot him a reproachful glance and told Sheikh Ragab to continue.

"The man died a few days ago. He died as a Muslim, leaving a son to his Coptic wife. I want to take custody of that child."

Nader Bey's back stiffened and he pivoted to face Sheikh Ragab directly.

"What connection do you have to the child that would grant you custody rights?"

"The father came to me to officiate the conversion, which puts me in the stead of the child's uncle. According to sharia, custody of a child should go to the parent or guardian of the best faith. As the father died a Muslim, praise the Lord, and as his mother is an idolatrous heathen, and he has no uncles by blood, we Muslims should raise him."

"Where the hell did you pick up that nonsense, Sheikh Ragab?"

"It's not right for you to address me that way, sir. And in front of those heathens who don't belong here. I have a degree from al-Azhar and I'm an official with the Ministry of Religious Trusts, which means I'm—"

"The word is either Christian or Copt, and they have as much right to be here as you and I do. And by the way, my grandfather was a sheikh at al-Azhar and my mother was educated in a school run by Jesuits."

The sheikh pursed his oily, fat lips and exchanged a knowing look with his servant, who responded with a crafty smile. He then reached into the folds of his abaya, pulled out a written application for custody, and set it on Nader Bey's desk. Nader pushed the application back to the sheikh and told him he could submit it to the judge himself, but that he would have to get his own lawyer. Sheikh Ragab started to object to the harsh treatment, but shut his mouth again when Nader glared at him.

The phone on Nader Bey's desk interrupted the tense silence. He snatched up the receiver and spoke in a low voice. Although I couldn't hear what he said, I could tell from his tone and agitated movements that the conversation had increased his irritation.

"Let's go," I whispered to Rizq. He turned to Nader Bey to ask permission to leave. He nodded. Whatever the source of his anger was, it made him forget to ask us why we had come to him to begin with.

As we left, I silently cursed Rizq for having dragged us to the prosecutor's office instead of going to Ramses. He was the only one who would understand our problem and do something.

"Let's go to the police station. Father Stephanos could put in a good word for us."

"Ramses has more clout here than Father Stephanos and the police department put together. Maybe the government too. He's more powerful than all of them. Just listen to me on this one so we can get it over with. I've already gotten to know this village better than you in only a few months, and you've been here for forty years."

Rizq shook his head slowly. He wasn't convinced, but he didn't oppose me either. He accompanied me to Ramses's place, although he lagged behind, taking reluctant steps. "Don't forget that it was your testimony that got Ramses locked for several days. Why would he help us now?"

He probably expected me to stop and give it some thought, but I ignored the question and picked up my pace. He repeated the question. I sighed impatiently and said,

"The whole town knows he stayed at the lodge during his detention. Also, I didn't mean to tell Nader Bey about that ledger. It just slipped out when I saw one like it on his desk. Anyway, believe me, Ramses is the only one who can help us with this. If he's a good Christian, he'll find it in his heart to forgive us."

"I still don't get it. What has your brother-in-law got on you? What can he do other than accuse you of getting married again after your husband died in Iraq? Why are you so afraid of him? The Lord called your husband to him, then you remarried another man of your own faith. Where's the sin in that?"

I had no answers to the questions he had been asking ever since I had shared my fears after Hilal appeared. Naturally, I didn't tell Rizq my brother-in- law's name so he wouldn't realize I'd been married to a Muslim. Very soon, I would reveal everything about Hilal and my marriage to Khidr, but only once, in front of Ramses. I needed him to intercede on my behalf with the Church. I couldn't wait any longer and I didn't have the strength to tell my story more than once. Even now, I wasn't even sure how I was going to start.

Nabawi Dib received us with a faint smile. In answer to my question as to where Ramses was, he eyed us suspiciously while tightening his grip on his gun.

"Why do you want to know?"

"We need to speak with him," I said.

"Personal visits are forbidden. Orders from Nader Bey."

Rizq stepped forward, peering anxiously behind himself a couple of times, and said in a low voice,

"There are these strangers in town and they seem odd. I thought I should tell Ramses about them."

The word "strangers" worked like magic. Nabawi's eyebrows shot up and a sweat broke out on his forehead as he looked past Rizq and scanned the road behind us. That password won Rizq new stature and gained us immediate access to Ramses' cabin. I left the mystery of Nabawi's sudden change of heart at the gate.

Ramses greeted us coolly. He didn't bring up his arrest and my part in it, and he was nice to Rizq, but he ignored me entirely. His creepy smile and constant bustling around the room made us both nervous. No sooner had we finished our tea than he got up to put the kettle on to boil again while he talked about treachery. Something in the tone of his voice made me hesitate, but I summoned my courage and told him I had come to him about a matter of life and death that concerned both me and my husband.

He swung to face me square on with a sneer. "Which one? Khidr—your first husband who, by the way, you're still married to? Or the second one, poor Rizq here, who trusted you?"

Rizq gaped at Ramses and at me. "Who's Khidr?"

I was too stunned to say a word.

"And what's this tune you're singing about life and death?" Ramses practically hissed the words, "Nobody died. Your husband—the first one—is still alive and as fit as an ox."

I felt unable to do anything but watch the changing expressions on Rizq's face, the desperate questions in his eyes, the strange pallor of his skin. I felt so nauseated; the ground seemed to sink and rise. I could not believe Khidr was still alive. What's the use of saying what I intended to say when Ramses put an end to all of it before I even began?

"Who the hell is Khidr?" asked Rizq, his voice hoarse. Ramses relit the small charcoal heater as he looked at Rizq with a malicious glint in his eyes.

"Traitors have no place among us," he said, "Your wife's an adulteress, Rizq. She's been lying to all of us. She's married to another man and to make it worse, he's a Muslim. Hoda ran away from this guy called Mohammed Khidr from a village on the outskirts of Giza. She hit him on the head and left him swimming in a pool of blood. Now his brother's looking for her here. God knows why she would do something horrible like that. She probably converted and kept that from you too."

Rizq gave a loud gasp, then collapsed onto the floor, unconscious, as if swept over by the avalanche tumbling from Ramses's mouth. I was being dragged under by the double onslaught of catastrophe and shame. Khidr was still alive, and I was about to lose Rizq. I was married to two men. One wanted to kill me and the other lay collapsed on the floor because of me.

I flung myself down on my knees like a madwoman and tried to awaken Rizq. I slapped him on the face several times. I screamed at him. Ramses reacted so slowly. He reached over to a reed basket hanging next to the window of his tiny kitchen and pulled out a large onion. He set it down on one hand and smashed it with the other, then held it under Rizq's nose. Rizq's eyelids fluttered slightly and his lips parted, but he didn't utter a sound.

"Call the police station and tell them to send an ambulance!" Ramses shouted at Nabawi, who was standing at the door, frozen. "Get moving, you oaf! The guy's dying here!"

Nabawi jerked into action and raced off. My tears flowed faster than the torrent of events. I tried to stand, but my legs refused to support me. I looked around, desperately. Ramses would not even look in my direction. He was done with me. He had detonated his grenades and hurled Rizq to the brink of death, shattering what was left of me. Even in the depths of this desperation, the image of Khidr's vicious face loomed before me.

At last, an ambulance arrived. Before we climbed in next to Rizq, Ramses turned to me and said in low voice,

"I'll let you tend to Rizq for now. But then you're out of here." His steely gaze bore into mine. "You're not welcome in this village any more. You should leave quietly before you're carried out in a coffin. If the people here find out about you, they'll tear your house down."

I pushed the wheelchair through the church gate, then around to the small side door. Rizq sat slumped, half asleep. It had been a month since Ramses struck like a scorpion, a whole month that we spent moving between the doctor's office, the village hospital, and a large public hospital in Giza. There still seemed to be no hope of recovery from the stroke he had suffered. Rizq had awoken from his coma to find himself unable to move or speak. It was impossible to know what he was thinking and to find the words to reassure him.

We passed down the long aisle between the wooden pews, then turned left. I now felt like a stranger in that building. My stomach knotted and I tightened my grip on the wheelchair to keep from shaking. My hand hovered over the door of Father Stephanos's office for a second, then I knocked and turned the knob without waiting for an answer. He held up his hand, signaling for me to stop. He approached, greeted my husband, grasping his hand between his palms, then patting his head and leaning over to kiss his forehead. He then edged me aside in order to take command of the wheelchair.

"You can wait outside until prayers are over," he said, with his back to me.

I tried to make sense of how he had looked at me—less with reproach or censure than with contempt. Hadn't I confessed to him my sins?

During that month when Rizq hovered at the threshold of death, I felt that God had vented his wrath on me for my lies by destroying all I held dearest. As soon as my husband was released from hospital, confined to a wheelchair, Father

Stephanos came to visit us at home. Now that I thought of it, he looked at me the same way then as he did now. I just hadn't paid attention to it at the time because I was so thrilled that Rizq was back among us.

"The Church has excommunicated you and annulled your marriage with Rizq because of your bigamy." Father Stephanos spoke with the same icy voice and stare that Ramses had used when he caused Rizq's stroke. He gave me a week to get my things together and leave Tayea. I'd had to take a seat for fear my knees would give way.

I had come to the church as a penitent and to plead for absolution. Father Stephanos refused, even though I was on the verge of abandoning my faith. I was an outcast on one side, and unwelcome on the other.

I left the room. As I walked down the nave, I felt someone behind me. It was a young deacon. He kept his eyes on me until I was out the door. Suicide crossed my mind, but I pushed it out when I thought of Rizq. Easter was in two days, so I decided to go to the market to buy him a gift. "Gifts bring cheer and make things clear," as he always said. I would buy him a length of fabric and have the tailor make him a new galabiya. I knew exactly the style that would please him. I was going to return to the church and no one would stop me.

My legs somehow managed to carry me to the market. The vendors were cold and hostile. As I browsed the fabrics on a cart, the vendor would say, "That fabric isn't for sale" or "Don't touch the merchandise." I began to lose my confidence. I tried to fight it, but I found it harder and harder to go on. Rizq had always warned me not to go to the Muslim markets, but his one was the closest to the church and a lot of Christians came here. I stopped in my tracks, suddenly alarmed that everyone had found out I had been excommunicated. Could Ramses have told them all so quickly? Or would the Church have done that?

I was about to turn back to pick up Rizq when I spotted neighbors of ours, Naguib Samuel and his wife Ferial. They greeted me cheerfully. When I told them about the trouble I was having with the traders, Naguib led me to a cart at the far end of the market street. Evidently, he was a friend of the owner. As Ferial and I began to sift through the fabrics and clothes displayed, I felt people's eyes boring into my back and I heard them whispering about me. One man had the nerve to stick two fingers up over his head in the cuckold sign. At least, it seemed Naguib and Ferial hadn't heard the stories about me yet. As people got bolder with their insults however, Naguib got riled up, and it wasn't long before he almost got into a fistfight with some of the vendors. Ferial and I rushed over to pull him away so we could leave in peace. We were only three to their dozens. Suddenly some guy pushed me in my chest so hard I fell on my back, which caused my galabiya to ride up, almost revealing my whole leg.

Ferial screamed and slapped her cheeks. The vendors pushed in closer. Her husband began to shove back, punch, and curse. They quickly got the upper hand and knocked him down next to me. They shoved Ferial down next to us too and began to hit us with sticks and hurl curses, some of them shouted, "*Allahu Akbar!*" while Naguib shot back, "Damn your faith!"

Just then a police siren blared. The vendors scattered like flies off a plate of sweets. The officers helped us to our feet and into the police van. We could barely believe we'd been rescued. We might also have been the first three people in the history of Tayea to rejoice at a ride in a police van.

At the station, Naguib refused to identify the vendors who attacked us, and they refrained from accusing us of insulting Islam. Ferial and I took his cue and said nothing. The pent up fury was so strong you could feel it about to erupt in a brawl right there in front of the officers. They released us all anyway, sending us all off with curses against our respective faiths.

I returned to the church in order to find Rizq. They told me they had sent him to his sister's, so I caught up with him there. As I related to him what happened in the market, his eyelids opened slightly and tears began to flow. I took both his hands in mine and kissed them, then I knelt before him and kissed his feet, and wept. When I looked up, he was still staring into space and crying silently.

Later that day, rumors began circulating like wildfire in the village and soon reached my door. "The Copts are poisoning the wells and they set fire to the Azhar Institute" went one; "the Coptic woman summons an evil spirit with the power to turn whole fields and barns of livestock into ashes in seconds" went another. I also learned that Tayea was ringed by dozens of trucks filled with central security forces and the police were letting no one in or out.

Danger stirred among us inside the village. Pick-up trucks mounted with megaphones patrolled the streets and told people to stay indoors. They addressed the inhabitants of each house by the name of the male head of the household, except in my case. When they passed my house, they addressed the warning to "Hoda the heretic." It stung. It was as though Rizq no longer existed. At least "Hoda the Copt" wasn't as cruel. No longer did they seek my benediction.

The noise of the microphones died down after a couple of hours. Only the crickets in the fields broke the silence. Then it started to rain firebombs. I had never seen anything like it. They whistled high in the air like red comets and landed on our rooftops or in our yards, without burning anything. I rushed out the front door to see what was happening. My neighbors were Muslim, but their house was plunged in darkness. The fireballs continued to flash and fade.

I rushed back inside to grab my headscarf and ran to Ferial and Naguib Samuel's place a couple of streets away. Dozens of men had assembled there. They were armed with hefty canes and some were loading rifles. I cast a worried glance at Ferial, but a warning stare from her husband kept her silent. He ushered the two of us into an inner room. As he shut the door, his eyes blazed and he nearly shouted, "Don't even think about stopping us! By the living Christ, we're going to get our revenge tonight. As God is my witness, we're going to dress them in their women's veils."

18

I SUNK DEEPER INTO MY chair. The monotonous tapping of the rain on the roof bored into my thoughts, triggering memories, making me want to plug my ears, "You've failed. They're stronger than you, stronger than the law. They are the law. Don't even try to resist. You're there to carry out their wishes. That's how it will always be."

Judging by the state of Ramses's room when I broke into it, that was where he spent most of his precautionary detention. Of course, I would never be able to prove it. The records at the police station say the opposite. The only one who seemed bothered by this situation was Nabawi Dib. His eyes spoke of a volcano bursting with molten truth, but he was the line that would help me hook my prey. I just had to pull gently at first.

I believed I could catch several birds with the single stone of Nabawi's testimony. In addition to Ramses, we could expose the SSI officer: I was sure it was Hazem Amr who was responsible for letting Ramses out of jail every night. If I could notch up the pressure on Ramses and unearth the missing agricultural property register, that would shed light into the dark corners of all those unsolved crimes. We would be able to name names and bring wrongdoers to justice.

But contrary to my expectations, the volcano behind Nabawi's eyes burned out, leaving a listless defeated look. I feared that whatever truths he held inside his chest would remain buried there. He insisted he slept too soundly at night to know who was coming and going during the time of Ramses's detention. That was odd coming from a guard, but what could I do? I had encountered yet another dead end. I had no evidence that Ramses broke the law and that the law enforcement officer assisted his escape from jail to the comfort of his own home every night.

My boss was forced to release Ramses on the fourth day. By the time he reappeared before me at the rest house, he had shed the defiant glint in his eye and the smugness in his smile. Unless I just imagined that. I was still dying to know what made Officer Hazem collude in Ramses's nightly escape from jail, but as he would never talk and I found no other way to find the truth, I tried to keep myself busy with other work.

The district police chief's office phoned me at the lodge to notify me that the house of a certain Halim Tadros had caught fire. A moment later, Officer Hazem called me on my mobile to inform me that it had been arson.

"Regretfully, the whole house burned to the ground with Halim, his wife, and five children inside," he said.

"And I suppose there are no suspects?"

That was a rhetorical question, but to my surprise, he said there were:

"They caught the guy while he was trying to flee the village. He's confessed."

"What's his name?" This time, the officer confirmed my expectations.

"Yasser Rashidi. He's a house painter from Giza, but currently unemployed."

I thought about the endless train of sectarian incidents in this little village. There was something unusual about this one. Rashidi was a Muslim, but he was a stranger to the village. What would compel him to set fire to someone's home with everyone inside? Someone must have incited him by filling his head with fanatical ideas. But why that particular victim? I huffed, impatient at how my questions only raised more questions. As I took my seat in the courthouse car, Nabawi Dib came over and hit me with a bombshell: the victim, Halim Tadros Iskandar, was Ramses's younger brother. Before I could catch my breath, Nabawi tossed a second grenade.

"Halim had just rented that house yesterday. It was the first night he and his family spent there."

"Who's the owner?"

"A livestock trader called Mohammed Hamdan."

As soon as I arrived at the crime scene, I asked Officer Hazem to bring me the suspect. Rashidi told me he was ready to make a full confession. I quickly examined his rather plump body for any obvious signs of torture. I had him accompany me so I could question him while inspecting the premises. I let him speak without interruption as he explained how he had poured kerosene over the front door and along the back of the house, and how after he set fire to the house, he stood back to watch, to make sure its owner was dead. In response to my question as to motive, his voice filled with bitter rage:

"That bastard Mohammed Hamdan stole my kidney."

When this news circulated through the village, it was greeted with a curious silence. The Copts weren't relieved by the fact that the crime hadn't targeted them deliberately. The

Muslims weren't interested in the stranger who came to settle scores with a Muslim they knew, but who had leased his home to a Christian, who died in his stead. To both sides the incident was like a 0-0 tie in a soccer game, with thoughts already turned to the next round. Tensions had been diffused, momentarily at least.

Still, I had to work over eighteen hours straight to establish beyond all doubt that Rashidi's confession was genuine and that Halim Tadros had not been the intended victim of a sectarian attack. If this had been the case, the retaliatory fires would have set the whole village ablaze and the bloodshed would have lasted for weeks. As a first step, I let some of the Coptic bystanders attend the inspection of the crime scene and made sure they heard Rashidi's story, which he recounted with venom. Evidently, Hamdan agreed to buy his kidney for 20,000 pounds. He paid a 1,000 pound down payment. Then, after the transplant operation, he wouldn't pay the remainder. He kept putting Rashidi off with various excuses until he stopped answering his calls. That was when Rashidi resolved to kill him. He didn't know that the day before he set fire to Hamdan's house, Halim and his family had moved in. Ramses's brother had found a job in the Tayea electricity company, which is why he had rented the house there.

I had Yasser Rashidi taken into custody for four days pending investigations. I then tried to find Ramses in order to pay my condolences, but I learned he had a breakdown during the funeral ceremonies at the church. The shock of seeing his brother's body charred almost beyond recognition was too much for him. According to Nabawi, Ramses thought of Halim as more of a son. He had a special affection for him and his children. Ramses himself had never married. Others said that, at the church, Ramses started to babble to himself out loud, as though possessed by a demon. One man told me, "It was the first time I'd seen Ramses without a smile in forty years."

Two weeks after the incident, Girgis entered my office carrying a large parcel. He set it on my desk, and stepped back to catch his breath, obviously winded from climbing the stairs with the heavy package. In answer to my questioning look, he said,

"It arrived at the post office yesterday morning. It was sent from Assiut, but the name and address of the sender aren't written on it. As you can see, it's addressed to you personally." Then he pointed to some large red lettering on the package that said, "To be opened by addressee only."

"Wait," I said as the clerk was about to leave. "I want you here when I open it."

Something made me uncomfortable about opening the package without a witness. Maybe it was because the public was breathing down our necks these days, waiting for us to slip up.

Girgis slowly unwrapped the package. Every strip of white paper removed revealed more olive green beneath, until, to my amazement, the missing ledger lay before me. I opened it eagerly and started to flip through it. I found many pages had been torn out, concealing evidence of the chains of deed transfers.

One name popped to mind instantly.

"Where's Ramses?"

"He's still on his two-week leave, sir." Girgis answered matter-of-factly. "He went back to his village to bury his younger brother and recuperate."

"What's his village?"

"Abu Tig, in Assiut."

Back at the lodge, I could still hear my boss's voice: "You need a holiday."

I thought about a trip to Cairo. Farida had been pressing me to come up for a short visit, but I found it hard to work up the enthusiasm. My mobile phone rang. I looked at the number and smiled. Speak of the devil.

She sounded unusually glum, and I quickly learned why. Her brother-in-law had been temporarily suspended, following his referral to the judicial disciplinary board, which would determine whether he was still qualified to serve. Magdi had been arrested for accepting a bribe from a wealthy businessman. In exchange, he had validated that man's title to a large piece of land designated by the government for reclamation by young agricultural entrepreneurs. It was one of the government's youth projects. With a flourish of his pen, Magdi signed off on 420 acres to a business magnate, and the next day, he had a neat one million pounds sitting in his bank account. Of course, he was unable to explain the source of his newfound wealth.

Not that this came as a surprise to me. I had expected this ending, although perhaps even sooner. Farida's sobbing broke the brief silence:

"You have to do something, Nader. Speak to one of your colleagues. He can't go to jail. He's from a good family. He won't be able to take the blow. Oh, and tell us, who's the best lawyer for cases like this."

"Okay. Try to stay calm. I'll see what I can do. Everything will be alright."

What else could I say?

I didn't dwell on the problem of my future brother-in-law for long. I set it aside with the hope that it would, indeed, end well—for the judiciary, that is. Fortunately, we still had the ability to purge ourselves.

I called out to Nabawi as I pushed open the door to the veranda and went down the steps into the garden. I decided it was time to ask him about that cross he had tattooed on his wrist, how he knew Ramses, and what had brought him to Tayea. I thought that a friendly session just between the two of us would loosen his tongue and ease his mind. He seemed to be comfortable with me now, especially with Ramses gone. As I took a seat in the garden, I decided on the direct approach:

"Tell me Nabawi, are you Muslim or Christian?"

"Time is my god, sir. He's the one that keeps me alive and who'll take my soul."

His answer left me at a loss for words. I asked him to make us some tea while I ordered my thoughts. I wasn't facing the lodge, but I heard his steps on the veranda, heading to the kitchen. I lit a cigarette and relished the smoke while I thought through my questions, testing them in my mind before I put them to Nabawi. I settled back in my seat and rested my feet on the chair in front me. Just then, Ramses's adopted dog bounded my way. I looked up to find that Ramses had appeared from behind me. He set the tray of tea down on the small table to my left with that familiar smile pasted on his face. Admittedly, something had gone out of that smile, as though it were a shadow of the original on his face for form's sake. I was about to ask him why he had cut his leave short, but he answered the question as though he had read it on my forehead.

"It's the mulid. Things get crazy around this time. I thought I'd better get back from Assiut in case you needed me if trouble breaks out. I mean, in the end, we've broken bread together, you and I."

What mulid—some local feast day I didn't know about? I wasn't sure things could get any crazier than they'd been since I set foot in this village. I nodded a thank you, then expressed my condolences over his brother. There was something odd in the way he looked at me. Maybe one day I would figure out what was behind that smile and get a step ahead of him.

Nabawi was now out front, guarding the gate. Ramses withdrew to the veranda stairs where he took a seat, lit a cigarette, and stared blankly up at the sky. His dog lay down beside him, panting happily. Nabawi approached and in a low voice pleaded on behalf of Ramses, who was crushed by his brother's death. He asked me to forgive Ramses for staying at his cabin while he was supposed to be in jail. He paused for a moment, then said,

"Him and me, we depend on your kindness and good graces, sir. I can't be transferred to another district and Ramses can't leave Tayea. We're at your service, sir. Whatever you say goes."

"So if I asked you to tell the truth, would you?"

He nodded. But that was after looking over at Ramses who, surprising me yet again, nodded as though he had heard every word we said. I postponed pursuing my questions as a frightening thought sprang to mind: could it be that Ramses had incited the murder and immolation of Alwan only for that to rebound on him in that horrid way? I doubted I would ever find an answer to that.

I went up to my room and changed into some casual clothes. I called for the car. I noticed my empty gun, and decided to take it with me. I got in the front seat next to the driver. When we reached the front gate, I had him stop and I called out to Ramses and Nabawi. In a voice that brooked no excuses I said, "Get in. I want to go to the village and see the mulid."

19

FERIAL AND I WATCHED FROM the window as Naguib Samuel
and his men split up into groups. Some headed in the direction
of the market and others to the southern farm or the Azhar
Institute. As their heavy footsteps faded into the distance, the
beating of my heart grew louder. I decided I had better go
home. Ferial insisted on accompanying me. Just outside her
house we spotted a band of bearded men speeding down the
street on three tuktuks. They were headed in the direction
of my house. One of the guys was waving a sword wildly in
the air. He warned us to stop where we were or he'd slit our
throats. Ferial shouted after him that he was a coward who
could only bully women. He leaped off the tuktuk and started
toward us, eyes flashing, bent on fulfilling his threat. Just then,
another tuktuk roared up from the other direction, U-turned
around Ferial and me, and stopped in front of us.

"Get in, Madam Hoda. Quick!"

As soon as we jumped in, the driver sped off. I looked
back and saw the man with the sword running after us.

"Hold on to your seats!" shouted the kid as he veered
sharply to the right and began to zigzag through the narrow
alleys.

The dirt roads were too bumpy for the tuktuk to get much headway so he knocked over a stack of chicken crates. The frightened birds flew up into our pursuer's face, clucking loudly. He flailed at the birds, pushing them out of the way and kept coming. Our driver honked his horn several times rhythmically. Evidently this was a signal, as several women poured buckets of water on top of the bearded man. He was undeterred, but the water must have made the ground slippery, because he eventually fell on his back. He gave up the chase but continued to pursue us with the hateful curses that spewed from his mouth.

We sped off, putting distance between us and the danger. The tuktuk driver still seemed very nervous. He was barely a teenager. Lowering my voice to a whisper, I asked Ferial who his parents were and where he lived. She shook her head, saying she had never seen him before. Just as I was about to ask him the same questions, he veered again into some dimly lit alleyway. We didn't see the ambush that lurked around one of the dark corners; we barely saw the flash of the blade before it pierced the fabric of the tuktuk's hood. Ferial howled in pain and clutched her side, which seeped blood.

The driver gunned the motor and swerved in the direction of the agricultural area.

"Where do you want me to take you, Madam Hoda?"

I took one look at Ferial and said,

"Take us to the church. There's a dispensary there."

He nodded and turned toward the church. Another group of men ran up alongside us and forced us to stop. Once they saw the boy's face, they relaxed.

"What's going on?" he asked them, feigning innocence.

"Some Copts trashed all the fabric vendors' carts in the Muslims' market. Then they set fire to some nearby shops," said one of the men.

"May God be with you," our driver said coolly. "I got two of the vendors' womenfolk here with me. One's been stabbed. I have to get her to a doctor quick."

Ferial and I hid our faces with our head coverings. She groaned as she rested her head on my shoulder. I feared the men would realize we were headed to the church, but our driver was clever.

"God damn those Copts who did this to her."

The men, reassured, flagged us on our way after giving the boy directions to the nearest clinic. After we drove some distance, the boy slowed down and turned to me looking deeply embarrassed.

"I'm really sorry, Madam Hoda. God forgive me, but I had to say those things."

I patted him on the shoulder. He gave me a shy, innocent smile and turned back to his driving. It struck me, for a moment, that his face seemed familiar, but my memory just wouldn't serve me in the darkness. As we approached the church, we saw that it was ringed by a convoy of pick-up trucks about 500 meters away from it. The boy slowed down.

"Keep going to the church. Don't be afraid," I said.

"Those trucks belong to Muslims," he said with a tremor. "If they stop us, they'll kill us this time for sure."

He swung the tuktuk around in a large arc. He momentarily lost control of the vehicle when one of the wheels slipped into the field next to the road, then he gunned the motor again and set us back on course. He drove as fast as he could until we reached a residential area west of the market.

To our left, several houses were in flames. A pick-up truck with a megaphone was coming in our direction, blaring out a warning to Copts to leave their homes before the Muslims burned them down.

Ferial was still bleeding, sweating profusely and groaning. My legs had begun to tremble so hard I couldn't control them. Masked men carrying lanterns were painting dark crosses on doors belonging to Copts. Others followed with cans of kerosene and torches. Constant gunfire rang out in the air. The boy pointed to the rooftops of some houses that I knew belonged to Copts. Armed men fired randomly towards a Muslim area. It was impossible to make anything out, but I was certain there were many dead and wounded among them as well. I prayed to Mother Mary to help us all, and cried silently.

I caught sight of Sheikh Ragab. He was at the head of a mob, commanding them to burn everything in their path. Suddenly, we found ourselves in an ambush. Men rushed out from behind overturned wooden carts they were using as barricades, waving their canes at us, shouting "*Allahu Akbar*" and ordering us to stop.

The boy slowed down, raised his hand in greeting, and called out,

"Hey! Guys! Praise the Prophet."

Since they thought he was obeying their order, they lowered their canes and started to exchange muffled opinions. Without warning, he turned and sped away as fast as he could. Just as we managed to put some distance between us and them, several shots rang out behind us. A bullet whistled past us and we screamed.

As we sped on, the driver slumped over the handlebar. We swerved back and forth, slid off the road into a narrow irrigation ditch and stopped. I scrambled out in order to examine the boy. He was bleeding profusely from his mouth and back. He smiled calmly. He was still alive.

I struggled to pull him out of the tuktuk and the ditch, and laid him on his back on the dirt road. By this time, some farmers from our side had gathered around us. They quickly got Ferial out of the tuktuk and one of them fired several rounds to repel the men from the ambush. What a surge of relief I felt when I recognized some of my Coptic neighbors. I urged them to rush Ferial, who had lost consciousness, and the boy to the hospital. I asked whether anyone knew who he was. No one was sure, but one of the men said that he looked like the son of Aryan the barber.

They lifted the boy and Ferial into the back of a pick-up truck and drove off toward the district hospital. I went with the others across the fields to the main church for safety. They assured me they had already taken Rizq there. In the light of the men's lanterns, we spotted several dead bodies in the fields. We went over to some to see if we could identify them. All of them had tattooed crosses on their wrists. One was Ferial's husband, Naguib Samuel. One of his eyes had been gouged out. I screamed and one of the men grabbed my wrist, pulling me away from that horrific sight.

"We have to keep moving," he said.

I followed in a daze, Naguib's final threats of revenge echoing in my head. My mind was a jumble of thoughts and feelings. What happened to the rest of the men who were with Naguib? Judging by our losses, the battle was going in our enemy's favor. Streaks of daylight began to appear overhead as we continued our march, silent, heads bowed as though in a funeral procession. The gunfire had died down. Armored police vehicles patrolled the town. The security cordons grew larger and tighter the closer we drew to the church.

Inside it was packed. Most of the Copts from the village were there, waiting for Father Stephanos to address them. Some were seated, others gathered in small clusters. I threaded my way through the crowd in search of Rizq until I found him in the back, alone. I pulled over a chair and set it next to his wheelchair. I took hold of Rizq's hand and felt a faint squeeze in return. It was the first reaction of this sort since his stroke. I turned to him and felt he was trying to smile. His mouth wouldn't obey the light in his eyes. I picked up his hand and bent to kiss the palm. That hand, though still frail, managed to wipe the tears from my cheeks and pat my head softly.

After nearly two and a half hours, the priest arrived. The scowl between the black *emma* on his head and thick black beard was so dark and furious that he was almost unrecognizable. He tapped the microphone to silence the angry murmuring. After some remarks about the grave events, he announced that his holiness the Pope would be coming down from Cairo that day or the next to comfort and bless us. The crowd rejoiced and cries of "hallelujah" broke out. He added that he had reopened the three churches that had been closed for a while. He stressed that the purpose was to shelter our community in this time of need. This was greeted with a loud applause.

We learned that twenty people had been killed. Nineteen of them were Copts. The sole Muslim among them had been killed by mistake. He had come across a roadblock like the one Ferial and I had encountered. Thinking it was manned by Copts, he turned around and fled. He sought refuge at the home of his business partner, a Copt. The men from the roadblock had caught up with him there and shot him dead just as his partner opened the door to let him in. They set fire to the house with everyone inside. They had assumed he was a Copt too.

Anger and grief filled the church. Everyone wore black apart from me. Even the cross on top of the church was draped in black. I had seen it flapping angrily as I entered. The story of the Copt who had sheltered a Muslim and then died with him moved some people in the congregation to relate similar heartrending stories from the previous night. One man related how, when his house was set on fire, his Muslim neighbors rushed over with a ladder to rescue him and his family from the roof. Others spoke of how Muslims had sheltered them in their homes to save them from the rampage. I couldn't help but notice that whenever people related how a Muslim helped them, Father Stephanos found a way to silence them, forcing them to furnish the remaining details in muted conversations.

I was also struck by how many stories were about Ramses. It was as though he was everywhere in the village that night, darting back and forth to help put out fires, rescue injured people, and transport the dead to the church. Father Stephanos said that the material losses came to hundreds of thousands of pounds, while the moral losses were inestimable. Dozens of stores were trashed and burned, people's homes were plundered and their furniture set on fire, many families lost loved ones—from breadwinners to children.

The priest spoke again, his voice hoarse and shaking with emotion. The groans of the injured echoed from the ceiling. Whenever a body was placed in a wooden coffin in front of him and cries of grief pierced the church, he stopped speaking. He gulped, then raised his voice in anger:

"Thank you, Muslims. I know you're listening from outside the church. I know very well who's telling you what we say. Thank you, those of you whose ancestors were Coptic Christians. With your fanaticism, you're making us believe what they say about you abroad: that it is your religion that incites you to hate us and shed our blood. I'm speaking about the religion some of your ancestors converted to a few centuries ago because they couldn't afford to pay the *jizya* tax on non-Muslims. Even though we're burying our dead today because of your extremism and intransigence, we refuse to believe what others say about your religion. We will forgive you, because that is what Jesus commands us to do. We'll forgive you because you're our brothers—"

His voice broke and he paused to wipe the tears from his eyes.

"But our Lord is watching and listening. Even if every official in the country does nothing, our Lord will act."

The applause rang out again and mixed with the weeping and wails of grief.

I spotted the two men who had taken the young tuktuk driver and Ferial to the hospital. I hastened to them to ask how my friend and the boy were doing.

"Naguib Samuel's wife is alive and well," one of the men told me. "The wound isn't serious. The boy died when we reached the hospital. His family was notified, and they came and took his body to perform the last rites."

Tears sprang from my eyes, as I prayed for the Lord's mercy on him and for solace for his family. I asked the man whether he knew the boy's mother so that I could pay my condolences. I added that the church could help her with her expenses now that she had lost her son.

The man looked down.

"His name's Hamada Islam. He's the son of Madam Bahiya, who lives three houses down the street from you."

Poor Bahiya. Despite my regret, a surge of anger clutched my chest. I snatched the microphone from the deacon, who was passing it around to those who wanted to address the whole congregation, and related how after Hamada had saved mine and Ferial's lives, Ferial was stabbed at one of our ambushes, because the guys manning it must have recognized Hamada and assumed his passengers were Muslim too. Then, while poor Hamada was trying to get us to the church dispensary, he was shot.

After I'd finished, Murid Dumyat, a neighbor of mine, related that when his son went missing, he called Father Thomas, the caretaker of the church, to beg for help because he was afraid his son had been abducted and killed. Father Thomas told him to be patient and pray. Fortunately, his neighbor Mahmoud, a Muslim, called to tell him they had found Milad lying in a field with a head wound, but he was okay. Mahmoud then put Milad on the phone to speak with him.

A woman with red, puffy eyes asked for the microphone. Introducing herself as Manal Zarif and speaking with a trembling voice, she said that several men she had never seen in the village before had broken into her home, killed her husband, and dragged her and her children outside. Just then, a Muslim neighbor of hers called Abu Qassem rushed over to intervene and managed to save her and her children from the killers. He put them in the care of some relatives of his who lived nearby.

Atef Blamoun, known to be a bigot, stood next to tell his story. With head bowed and in a low voice, he related how firebombs had set his house on fire, trapping him and his family inside. He called out to his neighbor's son, Ismail, who rushed over with a ladder, enabling Atef and his wife and children to climb down from the roof. Ismail then fetched his uncle, who had a rifle, and the two of them escorted Atef's family to the church under the protection of the rifle.

I asked for the microphone again but was told I couldn't have a second turn. Unable to contain myself, I looked straight at Father Stephanos, who was standing near the altar, and cried out, "There are two Muslims who were wrongfully killed, Father. Why don't you speak about them too? They died because they loved us. Yet you refuse to hear their stories. It's as though you want us to hate the people who helped us, yet forgive the ones who killed us. Our Lord is watching and listening to these good people too. How long are we going to go on saying 'us' against 'them.' Enough! Just let us live. I came here because I wanted to live."

Father Stephanos glared at me with undisguised fury, then made a signal to one of his aides and left. I couldn't tell whether the loud murmur in the crowd was for or against me. A moment later, someone approached and invited me to meet with Father Stephanos in his office. When I entered, I found him in the company of several bishops, priests, and deacons. He scolded me for interrupting him, then resumed talking to them about the virtues of forgiveness and tolerance. He then fixed his angry glare on me once again, announcing that the Church had annulled my marriage with Rizq because I was a sinner, adulteress, liar, and heretic. He ordered me to leave and never enter the church again without his personal permission.

I apologized for speaking out while he was speaking and asked for forgiveness, but he turned away and waited for me to leave. I begged for any punishment other than separating me from Rizq. He looked at the men around him, who stood as still as statues. I begged him to defer his decision until things calmed down and the crisis passed. Taking the silence around him as assent, he spoke, calmly, as though giving a Sunday sermon.

"The Church grants the sacrament of marriage. Marriage is a union that can only be broken by adultery. You are an adulteress and you left the faith when you married a Muslim. The Church is the representative of God on earth. It has the power to grant and to forbid. With the power vested in me, I forbid the continuation of your marriage to Rizq. I have granted him license to remarry should he so wish. But you, you may never marry again for as long as you live."

"How many times do I have to tell you, I'm not at fault?" I shouted. "I confessed this all to you. I don't want to marry anyone else but Rizq and I don't think he wants to leave me. I was forced to marry Khidr. I tried to get a divorce, but they wouldn't let me. When I married Rizq, I thought Khidr was dead. I swear by our Lord Jesus Christ, I thought he was dead. Why are you holding me responsible for things I can't control?"

One of the priests came over, took me by the elbow, and led me away. "Just listen for a second, Hoda," he said calmly. "If your husband made a mistake at work that caused his boss to reprimand him, and he came home and took his anger out on you, causing you to lose your temper with your daughter who took her anger out on the cat and killed it, which one of you killed the cat?"

20

We drove alongside the bridge for a while and then cut right. We found the mulid but couldn't see much of the countryside. The place was packed like the day of judgement. Excited faces, almost desperate to enjoy the festivities and escape their grinding poverty, unearthed delight in things as simple as an embroidered galabiya. To our left was a row of swing sets, each with a pair of swings shaped like boats. The kids didn't sit in them. They stood and used their full weight to force the boats as high into the air as they could, shouting and laughing at the thrill. I held my breath as, to my amazement, some succeeded in completing a full circle.

A little further ahead we came to shooting galleries. The reports of the light airguns were drowned out by the cries of joy from those who won little plastic toys for hitting the target. Hundreds of itinerant vendors cried out their wares. The din was so loud I couldn't make out what they said exactly, but most of them seemed to be hawking different kinds of fowl. The birds were bound together by their feet and could barely move a few inches on the rickety reed crates in which they were displayed. They bobbed their heads incessantly to the vendors' calls, as though nodding their assent to being sold for slaughter.

Most of the houses around me were rudimentary two- or three-story cement frames laid with rough red brick. Dirt roads lined with streaks of withering yellow did not bode well for the plant life. The unsightly chaotic urban growth spread relentlessly against a lush green, preparing to engulf it. It pushed back, but ultimately slowly gave way beneath the weight of the cement forest; it shriveled and faded, blurring the boundaries between green and gray, as the gray inevitably prevailed. Some of the buildings rivaled the palm trees in height. Unlike the palms, they were unable to sway in harmony with the breeze and crowded so closely around us that they practically deprived us of air.

I turned to Ramses and said, "Only half an hour ago, I asked you to show me some real rural Egypt."

He flashed me his ready smile. 'But here are the *fellahin*, these are their houses, and this is how they live. The whole village is like this now, except for the part where you're staying, sir. The *fellahin* of old you'll find in the novels you picked up from the bookshelves at the lodge."

In the distance, I saw a steeple. I asked Ramses what church it belonged to, but Nabawi volunteered the answer.

"That's the Church of the Seal of the Prophets, sir."

I burst out laughing, despite myself—the Seal of the Prophets was an Islamic title used for Prophet Muhammad. Ramses shot Nabawi a nasty glance and turned to me to explain.

"It's called Nour Church—the Church of Light. But the street it's on is called Seal of the Prophets. The Muslims in the village find it easier to use the street name to refer to it when they're giving directions. The Copts could never set them straight on the name."

To our left was a large stall with walls made of cheap canvas printed with bold arabesque designs. At the far end, an array of brightly colored Styrofoam toys were arranged on a long wooden table. Dozens of young boys and girls crowded around it, waiting their turn to take aim with the plastic rings.

The little boy inside me awoke. He rubbed his hands and stretched his legs, and I let down my guard and prepared to indulge him. I cast the protocols of my office aside and followed my inner child blindly. I won on my first throw, but lost on my second.

The boy inside Nabawi awoke, too. He shed his customary nervousness and caution, as well as the kufiya he used to hide half his face, and clapped excitedly as he watched. I held out three rings, telling him to try his luck. He snatched the rings with a spontaneity that took both me and Ramses by surprise. His first two throws missed his target. His third throw hit the game master straight in the face causing laughter all around.

I gave the first prize I had won to Nabawi and promised Ramses that I would give him the next one. He gave me a reproachful frown as he looked behind us nervously and urged me to hurry up. Some of the onlookers must have recognized us. Ramses was not the social type to begin with and the press of the crowds made him uncomfortable. I realized that the game master wasn't letting anyone else play next to me.

I got ready for a second round. The onlookers stood a respectful distance behind me, cheering on as I tossed the rings, applauding loudly when I won again. They urged me to take a third round and I hesitated. They were good people. Maybe they felt I was one of them and less like the other officials who intimidated them and brought them to me hands and feet cuffed.

Ramses bent toward my ear and said that, like any mulid, this one attracts more outsiders than locals. He was concerned for Nabawi's safety.

"With the hunter and the prey, the first to spot the other wins," he said. "Nabawi's the target in a feud and we're exposed here."

My mind pushed the ten-year-old Nader back inside me, and we returned to where the driver was waiting for us. I hadn't felt so content and carefree in a long time. I leaned back in my seat, closed my eyes, and slept all the way back to the rest house. Once there, I took a hot shower, climbed into bed and picked up the book I was reading. After half an hour, I yawned loudly and set the book down. I decided to phone Farida to catch up on the news about her brother-in-law. But just as I reached for my cell phone, I heard several loud gun shots in a row. They came from right out front.

I raced downstairs, barefoot and in my pajamas. Ramses was crouched behind the large sofa which he had pushed against the door. Bullets rained down, smashing glass, splintering the wooden door, flying through the windows onto the veranda and pounding into the walls.

"Get down!" Ramses shouted.

I obeyed, then crawled on my belly to the couch. When I reached him, he pointed to Nabawi, crouched behind a wall gripping his rifle and staring at the ceiling as though struck by thunder. There were tears in his eyes and he was muttering something frantically, but it was inaudible. Ramses explained that the people who had a feud against Nabawi must have seen him at the mulid and found out where he lived. Nabawi spotted them as they were coming down the road and raced into the main lodge to take cover. Ramses followed for fear they would kill him by mistake.

The guns fell silent for a moment. They were probably changing cartridges, because those were clearly machine guns. Ramses pointed to the cross on the inside of his wrist and signaled to Nabawi to show his tattoo to the people outside. He shook his head vehemently. Ramses whispered to him not to say a word or make a move and started to crawl to the phone to call the police station.

Nabawi turned to me and pleaded in a hoarse, desperate voice,

"Shoot at them, sir. By the Prophet you hold dear, use your gun. If you don't, they'll think we're unarmed. They'll riddle us like sieves."

My heart ached and my body trembled. Death was right at our doorstep and my inability to defend Nabawi with my unloaded ancient gun nearly destroyed what little authority I had left.

Nabawi started to move in my direction.

"Stay still," I whispered. Then, to assure him of my command, I said, "My gun's upstairs in my room. Don't move, Nabawi. I'll go get it. Don't worry, we'll do this."

Ramses managed to reach the phone and call for the police. But Nabawi, in his panic, bounded toward the stairs to fetch my gun. The second he moved, the guns opened fire again. Splinters of green wood from the shutters sprayed into the room. Nabawi's bear-like frame shuddered violently. He bellowed and blood seemed to gush out of him from all sides. He toppled backward like a huge tree onto the coffee table in the middle of the room, smashing the glass and wood with a crash as loud as a mountain caving in. The gunfire stopped at once.

I cautiously rose to my knees to peek through the broken window. Several masked men were racing westward, with Ramses's dog barking at their heels. I stood up with difficulty—my legs were shaking so violently—and went over to Nabawi. His back was propped up against the remnants of the table. Blood trickled out from his chest, mouth, and legs. He was still gripping his rifle with the same hand that had the tattooed cross on it. I collapsed to my knees again next to him. He looked at me with reproach before rolling his head toward his shoulder and closing his eyes. Gasping for breath, he pronounced the Islamic profession of faith. Then his grip on the gun barrel froze.

21

I SIGHED AND TOLD THE driver to switch off the radio. After a short distance, he veered sharply to the left, setting us on the highway to Cairo. After Nabawi's murder, I decided I needed a break to recover from what had happened. I had failed to help Nabawi, despite his faith in me. I let him believe I could protect him with a gun I had no bullets for. I deceived him. I was the one to blame for his death.

Three weeks had passed and I could not forgive myself. No amount of the customary adages and formulas about destiny and fate could console me or help me see things differently. "We all die in the end and only God knows when," people kept saying to me. The words went through one ear and out the other. We couldn't even seek justice for his killing. The perpetrators, as always, could not be identified. I tried to track down Nabawi's family but could find no trace of a wife or children. He died as he lived: alone, a stranger, afraid, and I could do nothing for him.

"Sorry, son, not today," I told the boy begging at my window as I rolled up the glass.

I was in my late father's car, an old black Chevy. Unlike the courthouse car, I sat behind the wheel in this vehicle. I drive with all my senses, as my father taught me, but at the moment, the road ahead was a blur. Farida was crying next to me, as she had been the whole way back from the High Court of Justice in Cairo. Her sister, Hanan, let out a loud wail from the back seat, shaking me out of my reverie.

We had just come from the first hearing of my future brother-in-law's trial. He had three of Egypt's top attorneys as his defense counsel. After the bailiff told us to rise, called the court in session, and asked us to be seated, the judge turned to the defendants to read out their various charges. Magdi stood behind in the standard white prison garb. Maybe some of those in there with him were criminals he had arrested when he was a police officer. Maybe others were suspects he had interrogated when working as a public prosecutor. To my surprise, he seemed to fit right in among them. He looked like them. He repeated the same phrases. As though taking his cue from them, he denied the charges and swore the solemnest oaths that he was innocent. He was as tense and nervous as the others. He spoke in outbursts, not sentences. His eyes bulged, his lips trembled, his hands shook, his whole body fidgeted. If he saw one of us looking at him, he averted his eyes and bowed his head.

Judging by his attorneys' arguments, there were holes in the prosecution's case big enough for a camel to walk through. The witnesses's testimonies were confused and contradictory, as though they had a secret pact to open the holes wider. After the third witness stepped down from the stand, Magdi seemed to relax. His shoulders straightened and the familiar arrogance began to creep back onto his face.

When the session adjourned for a break, Farida and Hanan rushed over to speak to him through the bars. I greeted him from a distance with a nod, before leaving the courtroom. I had my position to consider. At least to me that was a good enough excuse to avoid the dock and its occupants.

While I smoked a cigarette in an isolated corner in the hall, I pondered the state of the judiciary and my fellow members of that establishment. I wondered about his defense team: why would someone from the same agency as an official being tried for corruption step forward to defend his character and submit documents attesting to his innocence despite the fact he was caught in flagrante delicto and that it was an open secret in the agency that he had been abusing his office? They couldn't really believe he was innocent. And even if they knew he wasn't, would they still want him to return to work if the judge let him off? Surely they wouldn't think him fit to serve the public and uphold the law after he had sold his conscience. Perhaps they simply saw it was their duty to defend a colleague and gave it no further thought.

I pressed my eyelids closed, weary and irritated, and began to nod off. My eyes snapped open at the sound of a loud commotion nearby. A small crowd was pressing in on a man with a prominent nose and short black hair. Some of the people snatched at his clothes and shouted that because of his lies on the witness stand their son would spend the rest of his life in prison. They started to beat him right there in the court building. I shook my head mournfully then turned in the direction of footsteps on the granite floor. A loud murmur of voices filled the hall. My break from the proceedings in the courtroom had lasted longer than I had intended. As I would soon learn, the session had been adjourned again after only a few minutes, and Magdi's hearing had been postponed for another month so that the rest of the witnesses could testify.

Farida and Hanan were distraught. They had been so sure Magdi would be acquitted that day only to learn that he would have to spend another month in jail pending trial.

When we reached their house, I left the motor running. Farida invited me in to have lunch with them, but I told her I had to see my mother. The following day was the first of Ramadan, so I planned to meet up with some friends for the *suhur* meal. Before she got out of the car, I told her that I hadn't forgotten about how we still needed to buy furniture. My purpose had been to cheer her up a bit, but she dismissed my remark with a flick of the hand. Looking around quickly to make sure her sister was out of earshot, she then said resignedly,

"We'll have to put the whole thing off until Magdi's acquitted. I mean they can't convict him, right? It would be so unjust."

"Yes, God willing," I said, though I wasn't sure what precisely I wanted God to will. I let Farida interpret it as she wished.

"Unjust," I muttered to myself as I drove off. Who was the victim here? The young people whose land and rights were usurped thanks to Magdi? Or did he wrong himself and the rest of us in the judiciary by joining our profession to begin with?

Shortly before arriving home, I got a call from Mahmoud Bey to tell me about a deadly riot in Tayea. Dozens of Copts had been killed as well as two Muslims; one, a twelve-year-old kid. I said nothing. There was nothing to say. Even while I was away on leave, the village went up in flames. Evidently this time, the blaze consumed everything and everyone. Hundreds of Yasser Rashidis went on the rampage and set fire to everything, thinking this would vent their spleen. But fire always demands more fuel.

My boss cut my leave short. He wanted me to investigate the incident. "It's the best way to pull yourself out of the state you're in," he said. I had been on leave for some time, but I still couldn't get over Nabawi Dib's death. He had obviously decided to cure me with the same poison that had inflicted the endless despondency I had fallen into.

I called the driver and, at three in the morning, we set off, bound for Tayea and my fate. Ever-awake Cairo was still flooded in its bright lights, which we left behind once we crossed the overpass to the southbound highway and plunged into darkness. The driver honked even though there were no cars around. He laughed and nodded to the right. He'd disturbed two lovers furtively making out on the Corniche. My mind strayed back to the hell that awaited me back in the village, but travelling at this time of night brings on something akin to a drunken stupor. I stretched out on the back seat, alone with my sorrows, and wrapped myself in the comfort of darkness.

I sat up to get my bearings. The gentle breeze and approaching dawn made me lose my sense of time and place. The summons and the visions of strife slapped me in the face and put me on the alert. I glanced at my watch: 15 minutes past the hour. The light from the judge's lodge twinkled in the distance. The fields and buildings were still half asleep and careful not to wake anyone. They were unaware I had arrived.

I changed my clothes and headed straight to Mahmoud Bey's office. By the time I'd arrived, he had finished assigning my fellow deputy prosecutors their tasks. The task awaiting me was the examination of bodies in the fields.

He was feeling restless, so he decided to accompany me. Just as we were about to leave, Officer Hazem entered

181

the office. My boss let him know we were in a hurry and that we were on our way to inspect the scenes from the sectarian clashes. Hazem accompanied us to the car and then into it without waiting for an invitation. En route, he talked non-stop about the need for national unity and how our brothers the Copts were partners in the nation. I wanted to yell at him: the garbage coming out of his mouth was a mask for unadulterated bigotry and oppression. My boss nudged me with his knee, he must have seen my face reddening. However, when the officer started to speak about the Humayuni Decree on church construction and how the Copts might exploit the recent events—"like they always do"—to get a permit to build another church, I exploded.

"Humayuni! That's an Ottoman era edict. This is the twenty-first century, God dammit. So what if they build a church or even ten for that matter. What difference would it make?"

He was unfazed.

"Without that law, we'd have a tower with a cross on top next to every mosque. When we proposed to them the unified houses of worship law, which would have specified the number of churches and required distances from mosques, they rejected it. We're talking conspiracy here, gentlemen."

In Hazem's opinion, which he proceeded to explain at length, the Copts use a tactic of starting construction of churches without waiting for a permit, presenting the government with a fait accompli, and fueling resentment among their Muslim neighbors. It took some effort to interrupt him, to point out that Copts were the minority, that it would be easy to regulate the matter fairly, and that ordinary Muslims wouldn't run riot without a third party fueling ignorant ideas. He stared at me blankly, then got distracted by his walkie talkie. It seemed he was being asked to leave us and return to the police station. Some new suspects had been brought in and he would have to question them before turning them over to us.

We dropped him off. Before he got out, my boss asked him how many suspects had been apprehended so far.

"Investigations have identified fifty suspects. They are all being brought in for questioning. Twenty-five of them are Copts and the other twenty-five Muslims."

He cited the numbers with pride. I laughed and said,

"I'm beginning to miss the days of untraceable suspects and dead-end cases. It was so much easier."

The officer's face darkened. Barely managing to conceal his anger, he said,

"We're trying to strike a balance to keep a lid on the situation. Then we'll see. Don't forget, they have a lot of influence outside Egypt. The Americans heard about these incidents directly from Tayea even before we notified the minister of interior. I'm telling you that this is big. It's not just a case of a few fires and the killing of a few villagers. Our country's being targeted, so we must know who's with us and who's against us."

My boss gave me a sharp nudge in the ribs to keep me silent. He gave Hazem a smile and said something face-saving for us all.

"Of course. All will be well, God willing."

His smile vanished as he told the driver to get moving.

I cranked down the car window to let the cold air cool me down. The car moved slowly along the bumpy dirt road next to a large field. A couple of water buffalos and dozens of sheep were grazing here and there, rooting around for wild grasses to munch on. The exception was a donkey: his owner had removed his blinkers, attached him to a tree near a waterwheel, and set a large bundle of clover in front of him—the reward for his obedience. My thoughts turned to Sheikh Ragab, his mindless acolytes and his lethal diatribes, and it occurred to me that the donkey had struck the better deal.

We got out of the car at the eastern agricultural zone and descended the roadside slope into a field where fourteen murdered Copts lay. We were greeted by the medical examiner who told us that the victims had all been shot first. Their bodies were then brought to this field apparently so they could be incinerated in a large bonfire. Were it not for the fact that the wind was light, the bodies would have been burned beyond recognition.

My boss and I spent more than twelve hours examining the bodies and the crime scene. In addition to dozens of empty cartridges and fragments of firebombs, we found shredded identification cards belonging to the victims. By the time we finished examining the last corpse, the sun had almost set. We stretched and looked around. There was no one there but the two of us. We only had a large bottle of water each, so we broke our fast with a couple of sips. We would simply have to endure the bitter cold and the long trip back to the lodge for a meal that would probably not be very inspiring.

"Come break your fast with us, sirs!"

The invitation came from one of the conscripts who had been tasked with guarding the crime scene. He unwrapped a cloth bundle containing some loaves of bread and a chunk of cheese. He repeated his invitation with a friendly smile, so we knew his generosity was sincere and we did not hesitate to accept. He handed each of us a loaf and a large piece of cheese. As twilight turned to dusk, I noticed some bright green leaves in the pocket of his pita bread.

"What's that?" I asked.

"Radish greens. I found them right here in the field we're sitting in."

With a bright smile, he carefully plucked a bunch and handed it to me. I washed them off with the remaining water in my bottle, put them into my bread, and consumed my feast hungrily and with great pleasure. I prepared another sandwich and watched my boss pluck some more greens. Just then, three *fellahs* appeared, friendly faces lit by bright gas lamps. They were preceded by the village mayor who greeted us in his thick Upper Egyptian accent:

"Welcome gentlemen. You've lit up our clover field."

22

EVEN DEATH IS NO LONGER sacred. When Nabawi Dib died, the Church refused to perform last rites for him because his ID card, which stated he was Christian, was forged. Sheikh Ragab had already refused to perform the funeral ceremonies and let Nabawi be buried in the Muslim graveyard, also because of his fake ID card. The sheikh said he had nothing to prove that Nabawi had converted back to Islam. After shuttling the coffin back and forth between the mosque and church, Ramses turned to the deputy public prosecutor Nader Bey who issued a permit to bury Nabawi in the paupers' cemetery. Nader Bey and Ramses paid their last respects to Nabawi in that desolate place. The poor guy. He was treated no better than a donkey that kicked the bucket on the road. When the owner asked people what to do with it, they pointed to the nearest irrigation canal. No one cared about burying it.

Nabawi wasn't the only one to be kicked back and forth in death. Today, I accompanied Ferial to the police station to pick up the body of her husband, Naguib. He was just one of the many Copts who had been killed in the recent violence. To our surprise, we learned that the body of a Muslim was among the Coptic dead who had been assembled at Boulos Samaan's house before being brought to the police station.

As they were unloading them from the truck, a man bellowed, "He's Muslim! He's Muslim, like Father Stephanos said." In his rage, he knocked over the coffin causing the corpse to fall out onto the ground. I gasped and looked away, horrified by the sight of the burnt corpse. No one condemned the man's behavior.

Some people called up the church who told them to deliver the body to the mosque or the police station and leave quietly without causing any problems. At the station, Sheikh Ragab, surrounded by his men, crowded in. He refused to accept the body and perform the rites on the grounds that he didn't know the deceased. "He might be a Copt. This could be one of their tricks," he said.

We pleaded with the officer to just let us take Naguib's body. We had nothing to do with the Muslims who died, we pleaded. The officer was adamant that Sheikh Ragab had to take custody of the Muslim's body first and only then would he hand over the Coptic bodies. He then ordered all the bodies to be taken back to the morgue and for us to wait outside until the bodies were released.

Ferial wept. Other women wailed. A couple of men went to the church to ask for an intervention, but the church did nothing. Over two hours later, a car drew up and the medical examiner and other men got out. We learned that the brother of the deceased Muslim had come to identify the body in the morgue. Ferial and I bucked up a bit since at last she would receive the permit to bury Naguib.

I felt very tired. In recent weeks I found I could not stand for long. I saw a reed crate nearby so I took a seat on it. Then I saw Khidr.

I almost screamed. It was like seeing the devil in the flesh. I rubbed my disbelieving eyes and opened them again. He was getting out of a car just a few meters away from me. I tried to stand, but my legs started to wobble and my head started to spin.

"Hilal!" he cried. "God rest your soul."

I turned toward where he was looking. Hilal was the unidentified dead Muslim. Had the world grown so small that the Muslim carpet trader took refuge in the home of a Copt only to be killed there? And for me to find his brother Khidr before me alive and kicking? All because Sheikh Ragab had refused to bury Hilal.

Khidr saw me. A strange gleam shone in his eyes. Suddenly, he pounced and grabbed hold of my throat. Spittle spraying from his lips, he shouted,

"She's my wife! This Copt is my wife!"

The people around us thought he was a madman. They shouted at him to stop, which only made him tighten his grip. Some people hit him as they struggled to pull him off me. Others tried to squeeze between us to pry us apart, but failed. His hand squeezed my throat so hard I thought I would choke. Then Ramses sprang out of nowhere. He started to whip Khidr's back with a palm frond and swear at him. Khidr howled, but he still didn't give up. At last a police officer and some soldiers came out of the station to see what all the commotion was about.

The police wrenched Khidr off me and away from the crowd with great difficulty, then took us inside the station. People were clucking their tongues and shaking their heads. They had already formed their opinions and tongues were wagging about the scandal. Inside the station, Khidr only accused me of adultery. He did not even allude to how I had nearly killed him, but I could tell from the malicious glint in his eye that he was saving my punishment for later. He wanted to take revenge personally. Right now, all he wanted was to take me away from my husband.

He pulled his wallet out, extracted his ID card, which had my name on it as his wife, and handed it to the officer. His hand trembled and he was still panting. He wiped some spittle from his mouth on his galabiya sleeve and started to yell again, demanding what was rightfully his. That was me, body and soul, whom he had nearly just killed.

Apparently I couldn't take any more because I cannot remember what happened next. I must have passed out. When I came to, I found myself lying on a blanket on the floor in the district police chief's office. A Muslim woman whom I recognized to be a neighbor of mine, but whose name I could not recall, offered me some water and food, which I couldn't bring myself to eat. I suddenly felt a pain in my belly, but the officer refused to let me see the doctor at the clinic. He said I had to be taken to the night duty prosecutor first. Khidr was still yelling in the next room, threatening someone he thought had helped smuggle me out of the station.

The door opened, just wide enough for him to see me, and he spewed curses at me as several men pulled him back like a dog foaming at the mouth.

They moved me after nightfall. They put me in one police car, under heavy guard, and Khidr in another. I could not stop crying. When we passed the church, its steeple and facade with the large cross on top seemed so far away. Sorrow tightened its shroud around me. I could not hold on much longer. I felt I had lost my humanity, that my soul was seeping out leaving nothing.

Fortunately, the prosecutor on the night shift was Nader Bey. When he gave me permission to sit, I collapsed on the nearest chair. He reached for a ledger and opened it. But before asking me to state my name, age, employment and so on, he asked the clerk, Girgis, to leave the room. He then offered me a glass of water and, with a gentle smile, he asked me to tell him the whole story, off the record first. He promised he would not write anything down except my official statement.

I heaved a deep sigh, laden with the shattered fragments of myself and the pain in my soul, and said,

"There's no point anymore, sir. I'll tell you the truth for the record straight away. But I beg you to do one thing for me."

"What is it, Hoda?"

"If you're going to put me in jail, please get me to the hospital first."

"What's wrong? Are you sick?"

"I'm pregnant, sir, and Rizq is the father. Please, I'm begging you, don't tell anyone. Especially not Khidr."

23

She was seated on the bank of the Nile. A lantern set on the ground nearby cast flames of light on her black hair, which flowed down her back like strands from the moon. I was surprised to see her without her head covering. She seemed lost in thought as she stared out over the water which was as still as a mirror. The crunch of dried leaves beneath my feet caused her to cast an anxious look behind her. She didn't see me.

I hid behind the large trunk of an old tree and watched her from afar. I didn't want to spy, but I was transfixed. There was something about her I couldn't fathom. She had set the events in Tayea in motion when she arrived in the village, like the ghost of Nour. Perhaps. like history, myths repeat themselves. I felt helpless, as though an invisible barrier stood between us. They say horses have a sense of pride we humans can't understand. They never reveal their sorrow, never break under pain, and when the burden gets too much, they die, but they die standing. She rested her hand on her belly and shook her head, as though to allay my fears. Suddenly, she screamed as though in excruciating pain. The sound pierced my ears like an electric shock administered by an executioner. She stood, head cocked to the side as though listening to something I couldn't hear. She then took a wide swath of fabric, tied it around her eyes and stepped into the river. My feet sank into the mud, and I couldn't pull them out. My head throbbed, then everything turned black. I awoke to Ramses shaking my shoulder. I stared up at him, startled.

My biological clock gets inverted in Ramadan. I'm as busy as a bat all night, then in the daytime I feel as leaden as a sack full of sand. I got dressed listlessly. My enthusiasm for my job had been steadily waning as the end of the judicial year approached. My boss told me next year would be easier. I was not convinced. Some of the things I experienced in Tayea I didn't want to go through ever again.

As I went downstairs, I felt I was descending into a tomb. Today was Hoda Habib's hearing at the court of misdemeanors. I had no desire to attend the final scene. My nerves were frayed to breaking point, but I had no choice. I had never before felt guilty about a case. I could have turned this one down, but something spurred me to take it on, refer it to court and see it through the trial. It wasn't just curiosity or the desire to see justice done. It was to defend her right to live. I would probably be the only person in the courtroom to sympathize with her. The precise source of this feeling escaped me, but it continued to drive me.

I had done all I could to keep Rizq out of the case, but police investigators took the middle road. They said they were unable to establish for a fact whether or not he had known that Hoda's husband was still alive. Justice is blind and the law has imposed its edict by charging Rizq with complicity in adultery. The poor man had gone from life partner of a woman he had not known was still married, to a partner in crime in one of the most stigmatized offenses in the penal code. It would probably have been easier for him to bear had he been charged with murder. I did have the leeway not to detain him prior to the trial. It was the least I could do.

I found Ramses waiting for me at the foot of the stairs to the veranda. He saluted me as he approached and nervously held out an envelope for me. Before taking it, I asked him what was in it. He simply extended his arm further, the envelope trembling between his figures. He looked down as he did it, more out of remorse than respect, I thought. Curiosity got the better of me. I opened the envelope to find the missing pages from the agricultural holdings ledger that had been mailed to my office some months earlier. I flicked through the pages then lifted my surprised gaze to address the top of his head.

"And this came by mail?" It was a rhetorical question.

"No, sir," he said without looking up. He added no more.

I wanted to ask him about his connection to SSI Officer Hazem Amr. Was he the one who had let Ramses out of jail so he could spend the nights at the rest house when I had him detained? What did he know about the Copts' agricultural holdings, the arson incidents, and the firebomb attacks? But I found myself mysteriously at a loss for words. I uttered just a single word: "Hazem."

Ramses looked behind himself nervously, then nodded.

I folded the pages, satisfied with his answer to the question I hadn't asked. I climbed into the backseat of the courthouse car and told the driver to get going. Near the gate, I told him to stop. I turned around and signaled to Ramses, who came running. I examined his face closely, then asked, still tense,

"Is this the last of it, or is there more up your sleeve?"

"That's all there is, believe me. I promise to tell you the truth about the people who died, the Copts who killed them, and the land they took. Then whatever you decide, I'll accept. But, by Christ our Lord, I just do as I'm told. I've never hurt anyone or incited arson or murder."

"Get in."

At the courthouse, I took Ramses to Mahmoud Bey's office and told him to hand him the envelope and tell him the truth as he had related it to me on the way over. I took a seat and crossed my legs as he set the envelope on my boss's desk and stepped back awkwardly. I noticed a twitch in his right eyelid, but he seemed ready to accept his punishment, whatever it might be. He had changed since his brother's death. I had no doubt about that now. Maybe he realized that those he had depended on were no longer there to help him and that they had only ever been there to lure him into their service. Now he seemed free of those bonds. He just needed a last push to confess and atone for his sins.

My boss read through the missing ledger pages carefully then looked up, shifting his astonished gaze between Ramses and me.

"These pages were recovered from Ramses, right, Nader. He's the one behind the sale of all these properties to Copts, correct?"

I glanced at Ramses, whose hands were shaking while his anxious eyes were pinned on my mouth, fearful of what might come out. Turning back to my boss, I said,

"No sir. I received these papers today by mail at the lodge, like the last time. I brought Ramses with me here in case you want to ask him any questions you might have about the contents. He knows all the purchasers and their circumstances.

He has important information about some old murder cases. I think he wants to tell you so he can ease his conscience. One thing that's for sure, though, that envelope is going to be the last thing we get through the mail. Right, Ramses?"

The corners of his mouth curved into a hint of his artificial smile as he solemnly swore this was the last one.

I returned to my office, leaving Ramses to relate his story. Hopefully it would lead to the identification of some suspects from those many dead-end cases of arson and murder. I turned to the case folders on the recent sectarian riots. Each folder contained dozens of files and hundreds of pages of documents. I spread them across my desk in an attempt to make sense of them. We had questioned witnesses, interrogated suspects, and taken statements from officers and citizens who had "seen nothing." We listened to the grievances of the victims which only increased our grief over this piteous situation.

Tayea's Copts and Muslims fused into one. Crazed fanatics on both sides had turned their lives into an endless hell because they were bent on proving to their followers that the other side wouldn't get to heaven. As I leafed through the documents, the same questions taunted me: who had torn the spirit of mercy from one side and planted cruelty in place of love on the other? Where was the value in obsessing over others' prospects in the afterlife if you refused to learn how to live in peace in this life?

My thoughts were interrupted by three knocks on the door, reminding me of *les trois coups* before the theatre curtain rises. Officer Hazem strutted into the room. Despite his swagger, he looked like he hadn't slept for days. He plonked down on the nearest chair and rubbed his eyes hard enough to gouge them out, then looked at me with a startled expression. "If he's that rough on his own eyes, I wonder how he treats other people's eyes." I thought to myself.

"Order me a coffee, please," he said, taking a pack of cigarettes from his pocket. "*Ramadan kareem.*"

He looked at the cigarette pack in his hand as though wondering how it got there, then put it back in his pocket. He'd lost track of time, he said. He didn't know day from night or what day of the week it was, he was so bogged down in work. I let him vent his grievances for a bit, then interrupted him to ask the reason for his visit. I pitched my voice coldly because I had no desire for one of our long circular talks. To my surprise, he said he had some important interrogation records that identified the perpetrators in previous incidents. He carefully arranged some papers inside a red cardboard folder and set it in front of me. I opened it and stifled a snort. Obviously he had already heard about Ramses's confession to the deputy public prosecutor and realized he had to cover his hide. I flicked through a couple of pages indifferently, closed the file, and set it aside.

"Is something there not in order?" he asked.

"No, on the contrary. Congratulations. You've finally found Khalifa, "The Unidentified One" who committed all those crimes. I'm impressed. Here he is, first, middle, and last names and place of residence. Yet unfortunately, this happiness is incomplete. He was killed during a police chase in the mountains some time ago. But how could you have known he was Khalifa at the time? My condolences. May God have mercy on his soul."

Hazem stood, stifling a yawn.

"I've done my bit, sir," he said calmly. "The records have been turned over to you, and you have the guilty party. Those old cases are solved now. My role in this is finished."

"Great. Now what about the recent sectarian incidents? Are there no other suspects or is the late Khalifa going to be charged for those as well?"

He walked over to the window, pondered something outside that I was unable to see from where I was sitting, then turned toward me.

"I gave you two real pieces of information: Khalifa's full name and how he died resisting arrest, which led us to his ID card. So, there, that's the truth as clear as day."

"And a broken watch will tell you the right time twice a day."

Despite the sarcasm, the officer smiled for the first time since he'd arrived, then turned to stare out the window again. For some reason, it occurred to me to ask why Nabawi Dib had not been issued a proper firearm even though his life was at risk. He replied that the government had stopped issuing ammunition to ordinary security details in Tayea after a guard committed suicide five years ago and a central security conscript killed himself soon afterwards. Now ammunition was issued only in emergencies or for special missions.

The logic amazed me. He turned to look out the window for another moment with a mysterious smile on his lips, gave me a semi salute as a goodbye, and left without saying another word. I went over to the window to find out what had attracted his attention. I saw, in the middle of the vast field outside, a large scarecrow with birds nibbling at its head. It didn't make me smile.

"The court is in session . . . ."

We entered the court. I was a step behind the judge, and the court stenographer was a short distance behind me, following at a trot as usual. The "case of the Coptic woman," as the villagers called it, was the last on the docket for that day. The charge, as written on the case file with poor penmanship, was "Adultery by a Wife." It puzzled me that a woman who marries for love after believing her husband had died could be termed an adulteress, but the law made no exceptions for those who did not have their facts straight.

The place was packed to standing room only. Dozens of people were crowded into the narrow space between the last row of seats and the back wall. The villagers had been divided like fans in a football stadium: Muslims were on the right, Copts on the left. In the spirit of equality, roughly the same numbers of both had been allowed in. A cordon of central security conscripts was deployed in the aisle between them.

To everyone's surprise, including mine, the judge decided to hear Hoda Habib's case first. He had probably decided to clear out the courtroom as soon as possible. Few of the spectators would hang around for the case of Musaad, who was accused of stealing the water buffalo he shared with his neighbor and falsely claiming it was a bull so he could keep the milk for himself. Nor would the case of Abanoub attract much of an audience. He was suspected of stealing his neighbor's chickens by luring them with bird feed out of their pen and into his house, where he selected the largest to become a meal for his children. The defendant claimed he was innocent and blamed the chickens. Also on the docket were more violators of the onion cultivation prohibition. As mystifying as that law was, those cases were also unlikely to spark interest.

When the case of the "adulteress" was called, all heads swiveled toward the defendants' dock. She was in a prison-issue white galabiya and white head covering. She was gaunt

and gave Khidr permission to take a seat in the first row. He refused to remain silent and instead kept up a steady rant, most of which was incomprehensible apart from a stream of invectives against Copts. The judge ordered him to be silent and warned him that if he disrupted the proceedings again he would be charged with contempt and arrested. That worked, but no sooner did Hoda resume her account than we heard another disturbance in the back of the courtroom.

It was Rizq. He entered the room in his wheelchair, pushed by his sister. She stopped the chair halfway down the aisle. His eyes were fixed on Hoda, who returned his affectionate gaze. His attorney stepped forward to establish the presence of his client and present medical certificates attesting to Rizq's inability to speak. The judge told Rizq that he too could sit in the front row instead of the defendants' dock, but instead his sister rolled the chair to a spot toward the back. Obviously they had no intent of sitting near Khidr who looked back and forth between Rizq and the judge with an uncomprehending grin on his face. He then turned to stare again at Rizq and cast his eyes to the ceiling uttering loud imprecations. The judge was forced to issue a second warning. If Khidr disrupted the proceedings once again, he would be arrested for contempt and spend the next twenty-four hours behind bars.

I glanced at Hoda. Her eyes had widened in utter terror and her lips moved with a strange rapidity. Perhaps it was a prayer for Khidr to pipe down so he wouldn't end up in the defendants' cage with her. If so, it had the reverse effect. Khidr leaped from his seat and charged at Rizq like a bull that had slipped its tether. The guards managed to block him and wrestle him to the ground just in time. The judge ordered them to arrest him and lock him up in the dock. Hoda screamed and collapsed to the floor. Fortunately, the judge acted quickly. He ordered her released from the defendants cage then instructed her to complete her statement. She resumed her defense, with only some rusty bars separating her from Khidr and the predatory gleam in his eyes. For my part, I felt the spirit of justice had spread its wings above us and would at last bless us with a good ending with each party on the right side of the bars as they were now.

Concluding her account, Hoda said that she could have fled Tayea when she first spotted Hilal, just as she had fled her village so many months before. But she refused to be a coward and leave without ever being able to return. All she asked now was a fair trial for the first time in her life. She was sick of walking the line between dreams and reality and equality and injustice. Justice was all she sought. Fear was burrowed deep inside her. She didn't want to pass that on to the child she would bring into the world, she said, placing a hand on her belly and looking at Rizq with tear-filled eyes.

Just then, Khidr swore at her and tried to grab her through bars, but she leaped out of reach.

"That's my son in her belly!" he shouted. "She was pregnant when she ran away. I demand my right to my son and my woman!"

The judge managed to silence him with great difficulty. He then turned to me to ask what sentence the prosecution sought. I stood and cast my eyes around the room. I still found it hard to believe that all these people were here to prosecute a woman who had only wanted to live. Where did this lack of mercy come from? What was the source of resentment and malicious glee that feeds on the vulnerable? My role in this was about to end. Hoda's fate would reside in the hands of the judge, regardless of how I stood.

The judge cleared his throat, signaling for me to speak. I had apparently been silent for some time contemplating all those eyes pinned on me, daring me to defy what they thirsted for. But I could not bring myself to reiterate the usual formula at the end of a hearing: "The prosecution rests and asks the court to uphold the charges." I swallowed, as though gulping for air. I raised my voice loud enough for Hoda to hear and said, "The prosecution defers to the court."

The judge looked at me with raised eyebrows, but said nothing. The lawyer appointed to defend Hoda was practically jumping for joy as he stood to give his closing argument. What I had just said meant that the prosecution requested an acquittal or as light of a sentence as possible and that it was now up to the judge to show the mercy and compassion the prosecution could not.

When I sat down, my forehead was dripping with sweat even though I had only said a few words. After hearing the plea from Rizq's lawyer, the judge closed his case file. I think my heartbeat paused as he looked first at Khidr and Rizq, and then at Hoda. He called her name in a low voice. She stood. Then in a voice loud enough for the all in the room to hear, he said,

"I will pronounce the verdict at the end of the session."

24

I HESITATED, THEN GENTLY SET my hand on Rizq's open palm. His feeble fingers closed around mine as he turned his head slowly toward me. His trembling lips struggled to form a smile.

I leaned my head toward him and whispered, "I didn't know that Khidr was still alive. I didn't mean to kill him."

Rizq nodded, holding that faint smile in place to reassure me.

How my heart ached for the suffering I had caused him. How it had pained me that I had not been able to tell him the whole truth like I told the deputy public prosecutor. In order to get out of the charge of adultery, I had to admit that I had tried to kill Khidr and that I truly believed he had died, for otherwise I would never have married Rizq.

After hearing my confession, Nader Bey looked at me with astonishment, but he did not record a word of what I had told him. He simply wrote that I denied having committed the crime of adultery and omitted the rest.

That day in court, when Nader Bey stood and told the judge he deferred to the court, my heart sank. Why did he change his mind and leave us to the mercy of the judge? Why didn't he say a word in our defense? Did he want to leave the slaughter to others so he wouldn't have our blood on his hands? I found that hard to believe.

When he left the room behind the judge, head bowed, was that in sorrow or remorse? I had no idea what was going on around me. The courtroom was in uproar. It was like the village market. Everyone was shouting at once. No one listened to what others had to say; faces were pinched and arms gesticulated wildly.

Instead of ordering me back in the defendants' cage, the judge allowed me to stay with Rizq under guard. We were sitting together in the back of the room. On my right stood a skinny police conscript, yawning so often that I thought he might fall asleep on his feet. His colleague stood on Rizq's left, slouching lazily against the wall. They knew we were not going to escape. We were cordoned off from the rest of the courtroom by over ten central security forces in black uniforms, all armed with billy clubs. They stood in front of us, arms interlocked, creating a thick human chain and a fence between us and the villagers. We were physically kept apart, but the distance had long existed, even if we pretended otherwise.

"Court is in session!"

The bailiff's bellow sounded like a threat, but it inspired awe. We all stood, except for Rizq, of course, as the judge took his seat. Nader Bey still seemed tense as he took his seat to the far right.

My fingers slipped from Rizq's hand. They'd grown clammy. But he kept his palm open and looked into my eyes, so I returned my hand to his and he covered it with his other hand. Without looking up, the judge called out my name first, then Rizq's. Fixing his eyes toward a spot in the middle of the room, he said in a stern voice,

"The court rules in the presence of the defendant to acquit Rizq Alfi Hakim of the charge brought against him and to sentence the defendant Hoda Yusef Habib to a year with labor and a fine of one hundred pounds— "

The judge paused for a moment. It seemed longer than that, but no one dared violate its sanctity. Then he added,

"—with a stay of execution."

I could no longer live in the shadows. I spent my whole life on the fringes of happiness and security, always on the run from one specter or another. Poverty, cruelty, injustice, persecution— they never ceased to nip at my heels. Why did fate treat me like a tumbleweed, a toy for the winds to toss back and forth? I would be better off as a stone; I would at least have stability.

I was alone, an outcast. If I encountered anyone in the street, I'd avert my eyes and hope to disappear. I was afraid of what people might say or do, even if they only caught sight of my reflection in a window or saw my shadow pass beneath a street lamp. I was worn to the bone from the constant humiliation and had nothing to drown my sorrows in. The only person who would put me up was Nader Bey. He let me stay in the little hut next to Ramses's cabin. It was where Nabawi Dib stayed, before it became a refuge for strangers and strays.

I needed a change of air. I left the grounds and crept between the trees and shrubbery behind the lodge, with Ramses's dog following silently. At least he didn't feel I was an alien. He didn't growl or snarl, so maybe he had come along to comfort me. I sat on the edge of the river, letting the water lap at my feet. The Nile's tiny waves calmly broke near the bank. They humbly rose and bowed in prayer to their Creator. They sighed as though whispering their last wishes before they died back down. I erupted into hysterical laughter. I cried and wailed, gripping my head between my hands to keep it from exploding.

I fled to this sacred river to cleanse myself in its water, to leave my sorrows with it and shed my pain. After the judge pronounced his ruling, time seemed to stop and the deafening noise was put on mute. The crowd—arms flailing, mouths twisted around hateful words, eyes emitting sparks of malice—receded into the distance, leaving me suspended in space, alone. I have no one left but you, dear Virgin Mary, Mother of the Light. Please don't forsake me. I am a stranger, abandoned by all and lost in this world. It takes faith in oneself to find one's way back, and that I have never found.

A strange air of expectancy hovered around me; even the tree leaves had stopped rustling. I picked up a flat stone, weighed it in my hand and flicked it over the water. It skipped a few times, confident it could hop to the other side, then sank. Ramses's dog wagged his tail and sat next to me. The solar disk, reddening out of shyness or fright, was slowly dipping into the Nile. I placed my hand on my swollen belly. The Lord had finally blessed me with a child. Maybe it would be a boy. That had been Hilal's worst fear. He couldn't stand the thought of Khidr having a son and heir from his Coptic wife. Hilal died before he could inherit anything and the father of this child was not Khidr, but Rizq, who had waited so long for the Lord to reward his patience. Rizq had waited until his health ailed and he had been separated from me.

This poor child! To be born into such a cruel world.

I still couldn't believe what I saw after my release. I asked the sergeant assigned to guard me to take me to my old house. "The Coptic woman's house," I told him and smiled. It was the first time I used that name. The sergeant's eyes widened and he did not return the smile. He pulled out a large white handkerchief and looked down as he wiped the sweat from his brow. He was avoiding my gaze. I had to repeat my request several times before he finally agreed. He warned me that my house had been half-demolished while I was in detention in the prison hospital.

The roads looked the same, but people's faces and their very souls had changed, forcing me to block my ears and blinker my eyes as I stumbled behind my guard. It was exactly as he said. Half the house had been razed to the ground and turned to rubble. The other half had been pummeled with mallets. Cracks and fissures zigzagged up the walls like snakes, devouring my memories.

"The Coptic woman's house" was once akin to a shrine for both Muslims and Copts. They circumambulated it, pressed their hands and faces to the walls, and uttered prayers petitioning for my blessing. Then they had torn it down, trampled on it, and cursed it and me as wicked and impure.

According to the sergeant, the government ordered several houses belonging to Copts demolished, not just mine. I knew mine was in full compliance with the building codes. Rizq had never broken a law in his life.

Rizq had to leave the house and go live with his sister Sara. It was too risky for him to have me visit him there, so he asked to meet me secretly, away from the prying eyes of the villagers and, more importantly, the church. Rizq had forgiven me from his heart. That was my sole comfort. Sara told me he planned to convert to Islam so he could marry me again after I win my divorce from Khidr. Rizq was as much of a wreck as I was. We were both waiting for the torrent of hatred to sweep us away, which seemed only a matter of time.

I watched the waves break beneath the moonlight. How they resembled my life: bursts of hope interrupted. Whenever I felt happiness was in reach, it evaporated before I could hold it in my grasp. Fear always snuffed out the flickers of freedom I had. I stood up, took off my galabiya and undid my braids. It was time to go into the river. The dog stood up, alert. I patted him on the head to reassure him. I would stay near the bank because I couldn't swim, with the current or against it. I would never surrender to anyone again. I may not have been able to choose the life I wanted, but today I could choose the ending. At least I would have exercised my own free will.

I stepped into the water up to my shoulders. I closed my eyes. I was happy with my decision. I would have a new home here. I would never leave Tayea, forever.

25

THE REST OF THE YEAR had passed without incident. The villagers must have satisfied their need for trouble with all that they had caused and experienced, and decided to call a truce.

A couple of days before my last day in Tayea, Ramses woke me to tell me Hoda had gone into labor, two months prematurely. I phoned my boss to make the arrangements to take her to the hospital and had my driver take her there before dawn while the village was still asleep.

I was too busy to visit her later that day. I had just received notification of my transfer and I was working to close as many cases on my docket as possible. I spent the whole night in my office. At the first rays of dawn I stretched out on the couch and closed my eyes. The church bells woke me two hours later. They had been silent for several weeks. They peeled loudly from the tallest spire and were echoed by the bells in the three other churches that had been reopened. I returned to the lodge and dragged myself upstairs to my bedroom, yawning and longing for sleep. Then I stopped at the sight of a small gold cross hanging from a chain on the headboard. I turned to Ramses who had followed me upstairs, head bowed.

"It's Hoda's. She forgot to take it with her when we rushed her to the hospital." Then his voice broke. "She didn't make it, sir. I'm sorry."

I was too stunned to move as he continued, eyes brimming with tears.

"Hoda died in the hospital after giving birth. She lost a lot of blood, and they couldn't find a single donor for her."

I stared at his grieving face, unable to think of a word to say. She had died so suddenly, leaving us in shock. She departed this world before seeing what she had lived for. All those people who refused to donate blood were no better than the unidentified criminal who had murdered one of us every day, before our very eyes.

I took hold of the cross, then put it back. My reality had dissolved my dreams, like it always does. Perhaps the greatest sacrifice I can make in these wretched times is to reconcile myself to what I am helpless to prevent. Only then can I hold on to my love for life. My eyes welled as I turned to pack, tossing items into my suitcase in no particular order. Before leaving the room, I returned to the headboard, took the cross and put it in my pocket. Downstairs, I returned the two volumes by Tawfiq al-Hakim to the bookshelf exactly where I found them: between two large leather-bound books where no one would spot them easily. I had no more use for them and others might be pleased to see that nothing at all had changed.

I turned to Ramses, who was carrying my suitcase, and asked, though I was afraid to hear the answer:

"Did Hoda give birth? Or did the child die too?"

"She had twins, sir. She asked me to name them Nader and Kamal. But the hospital refused to record the name of the father. Khidr has filed a lawsuit against her. He claims he's the father. But he left the village today. Actually, he ran away."

"Why? What's he afraid of?"

"He's got a duty to avenge his brother, who was killed by those fanatics. But they threatened him, so he took off, the coward. He didn't even stay long enough to bury Hoda and to see the twins. May God have mercy on us all." Ramses swallowed with difficulty, either to fight back his tears or keep from spitting. "I hope he rots in hell, and soon!"

I packed up the rest of my belongings at the office, except for the desk set Farida had given me. I then met with the deputy public prosecutor who had been appointed to replace me. It was clear he was eager to get started and "take up the torch of justice," as he put it. I wished him the best of luck and added, with a bitter smile, "You'll need it."

He looked at me in surprise, but let it drop. He held up a small sheaf of papers—a notice regarding a new police investigation and some accompanying documents—and asked for advice. Was this something he should show to the district public prosecutor first before going to the scene to investigate? A laborer called Mohammed Semeida had been found dead, his belly slit open, in an irrigation ditch.

"Have they found any suspects?" I asked indifferently.

"According to the police inquiries so far, he was killed following a fight in a coffeehouse with a certain Ahmed Komi, a farmer. It was about a dispute over—"

"So it's an Ahmed kills Mohammed case. That's routine. It happens every day around here. Just tell your boss about the important cases."

Before taking my leave of Tayea, I paid a last visit to Nabawi Dib in the paupers's graveyard. He was buried with the others who had no family to claim them, and no religion either, in his case. It was the last errand I had assigned myself after I received notification of my transfer. It was sudden, but not extraordinary; it was just part of the judiciary's schedule of appointments and tour rotations for the next year. My new post was far away from Cairo, in Aswan, the southernmost prosecution circuit in the country. Mahmoud Bey was transferred as well, to Alexandria, as though they wanted to make sure that we were as far apart as possible now that we had become friends.

I sat in the car, newspaper on my lap, staring out the window. The road workers were as busy as an army of ants, laying and rolling the asphalt in preparation for the following day's visit by some second-tier government technocrats and National Democratic Party leaders. They were coming to speak to local officials about "the reform of religious discourse," as was reported in the national dailies, citing President Hosni Mubarak's appeal.

I picked up the newspaper and flipped through the pages with little interest. Mubarak's statements had been transformed into lengthy op-eds, all nearly identical versions of each other. The state-appointed editors-in-chief had been given the same talking points, and they all concluded that tomorrow brings a "brighter day." I shook my head at our sad condition. We acted emotionally, on the spur of the moment, and everything was ad hoc, short term. Nothing stood a chance to grow, apart from the seeds of strife.

The past months seemed like a single long, dismal, and brutal night. Now I felt I was approaching day or, at least, the first tentative rays of light appeared from afar. I turned to look out of the rear window. We had left the roadworks behind us. The faded sign with the name of the village, "Tayea," lay on the ground, like a corpse. The construction workers trampled on it as they planted a new sign, as per instructions. It bore the government's new chosen name: "Peace Village."

Returning to my newspaper, I noticed a small headline in the "Crime and Accidents" section: "The district criminal court has acquitted all defendants in the Tayea riots case." Not a single Copt or Muslim was found guilty of all those acts of murder, maiming, arson, theft and plunder. Talk about a dead-end case. Apparently, with Khalifa dead, they had to wait for a new scapegoat.

We passed the "Coptic woman's house." I would not have known had the driver not pointed it out. I asked him to slow down and drive around it. The wide wooden door lay on the ground amid the rubble. It was covered with dust, but I could still make out a black cross painted on it. If only Hoda had held out a little longer. Fate sometimes saves good surprises for the very end, just as we succumb to despair. Khidr had fled, and Rizq was getting better. If only fate had given her one last chance.

Just west of the village, we turned right toward the entrance of the paupers's graveyard. To my surprise, there were several central security trucks and dozens of riot police. My phone buzzed, announcing an SMS from Farida. Magdi had been acquitted and would return to work in a few days, she wrote, punctuating it with exclamation marks and a smiley. When would I be returning to Cairo so we could finish equipping our flat? More smileys. I then noticed five missed calls from her. I hadn't heard the phone ring. I erased the SMS and put my phone on silent. I pulled out my gun, contemplated its empty chamber for a moment, then grunted and returned it to its holster at my side. I had wanted to use it, but couldn't. I picked up my phone again, typed a short message to Farida and pressed send. I emitted a long sigh of relief.

I asked one of the officers the reason for all the security. He said that Hoda Habib was about to be buried and they feared a disturbance. The church had excommunicated her and Sheikh Ragab had initially refused to have anything to do with her burial, until Khidr signed a sworn statement that she had converted to Islam orally. I felt like saying, if only they had assigned half as many police to protect her while she was still alive, she wouldn't have had to live a thousand deaths among us.

I moved to a corner at the other end of the courtyard and recited the Fatiha over the soul of poor Nabawi Dib. He had been like an extra in a film, someone the audience forgot as soon as the scene changed. Feeling the tears well in my eyes, I turned away so no one would see me.

A sudden commotion drew my attention to the entrance. Outside, some stray sheep and goats moved out of the way. Police rushed to form a cordon, separating me from the others. Hoda's coffin had arrived. Sheikh Ragab took a spot next to the district police chief and delivered a perfunctory service. He called for God to forgive the sins of the deceased, but not once did he utter the word "mercy." He recited some short Quranic verses which he had obviously selected with great care from surat al-Tawbah. They were all about "repentance." They had a sheikh known for inciting hatred against Copts perform the last rites for the person people called the Coptic woman.

The silence of the graves enveloped us, despite the many people present. I turned at the sound of someone behind me stifling a cry. It was Rizq in his wheelchair, head bowed. Behind him, Ramses pushed the chair slowly. Hoda's husband had aged years in only a few months. Our eyes met in silence. I went over to him, pulled Hoda's golden cross from my pocket, placed it in his palm, and closed his fingers around it. I averted my face as my eyes welled again and his trembling shoulders rent my heart.

Before leaving, Ramses and I exchanged a parting look. That morning, I learned that the prosecutor's office had opened an extensive investigation into the agricultural arson incidents, the suspicious suicides from rooftops, and the tampering with property ownership documents. Naturally, he was a prime suspect, but he hadn't been called in for questioning yet.

There was strange, almost deathlike, repose in his face and a faraway look in his wide eyes. There was not even a trace of a smile.

Just as I was about to get into the car, I noticed Rizq's sister with some other women from the village. Their wailing grew louder as I approached, drowning out the cries of Hoda's twins. I was unable to see their faces. I could only make out tiny wriggling shapes swaddled in black. But I knew they had inherited a heavy legacy of hardship and persecution. Already they waited for a judge to determine who the father was: Rizq or Khidr.

I turned to leave, struggling with questions I would never be able to answer. I left Tayea behind me with prayers for mercy for Hoda Habib, whom we had killed simply because she wanted to live.